ACCLAIM FOR THE NOVELS OF
LEILA MEACHAM

TITANS

"The novel has it all: a wide cast of characters, pitch-perfect period detail, romance, plenty of drama, and skeletons in the closet (literally). Saga fans will be swooning."

—*Booklist* (starred review)

"It has everything any reader could want in a book...epic storytelling that plunges the reader headfirst into the plot... [Meacham] is a titan herself." —*Huffington Post*

"Emotionally resounding...Texas has never seemed grander... Meacham's easy-to-read prose helps to maintain a pace that you won't be able to quit, pushing through from chapter to chapter to find the next important nugget of this dramatic family tale. It is best savored over a great steak with a glass of wine and evenings to yourself." —BookReporter

SOMERSET

"Bestselling author Meacham is back with a prequel to *Roses* that stands on its own as a sweeping historical saga, spanning the nineteenth century...[Fans] and new readers alike will find themselves absorbed in the family saga that Meacham has proven—once again—talented in telling."

—*Publishers Weekly* (starred review)

"Entertaining...Meacham skillfully weaves colorful history into her lively tale...*Somerset* has its charms."

—*Dallas Morning News*

"Slavery, westward expansion, abolition, the Civil War, love, marriage, friendship, tragedy, and triumph—all the ingredients (and much more) that made so many love *Roses* so much—are here in abundance." —*San Antonio Express-News*

"A story you do not want to miss...[Recommended] to readers of Kathryn Stockett's *The Help* or Margaret Mitchell's *Gone with the Wind*. *Somerset* has everything a compelling historical epic calls for: love and war, friendship and betrayal, opportunity and loss, and everything in between." —*BookPage*

"4½ stars! This prequel to *Roses* is as addictive as any soap opera...As sprawling and big as Texas itself, Meacham's epic saga is perfect for readers who long for the 'big books' of the past. There are enough adventure, tears, and laughter alongside colorful history to keep readers engrossed and satisfied."

—*RT Book Reviews*

TUMBLEWEEDS

"[An] expansive generational saga...Fans of *Friday Night Lights* will enjoy a return to the land where high school football boys are kings." —*Chicago Tribune*

"Meacham scores a touchdown...You will laugh, cry, and cheer to a plot so thick and a conclusion so surprising, it will leave you wishing for more. Yes, Meacham is really that

good. And *Tumbleweeds* is more than entertaining, it's addictive."
                                                        —Examiner.com

"If you're going to a beach this summer, or better yet, a windswept prairie, this is definitely a book you'll want to pack."
                                        —*Times Leader* (Wilkes-Barre, PA)

"[A] sprawling novel as large as Texas itself."
                                                        —*Library Journal*

"Once again, Meacham has proven to be a master storyteller... The pages fly by as the reader becomes engrossed in the tale."
                                        —*Lubbock Avalanche-Journal* (TX)

ROSES

"Like *Gone with the Wind*, as gloriously entertaining as it is vast... *Roses* transports."
                                                        —*People*

"Meacham's sweeping, century-encompassing, multigenerational epic is reminiscent of the film *Giant*, and as large, romantic, and American a tale as Texas itself."
                                                        —*Booklist*

"Enthralling."
                                        —*Better Homes and Gardens*

"The story of East Texas families in the kind of dynastic gymnastics we all know and love."
                                                        —Liz Smith

"Larger-than-life protagonists and a fast-paced, engaging plot... Meacham has succeeded in creating an indelible heroine."
                                                        —*Dallas Morning News*

"[An] enthralling stunner, a good, old-fashioned read."

—*Publishers Weekly*

"A thrilling journey…a treasure…a must-read. Warning: Once you begin reading, you won't be able to put the book down."

—Examiner.com

"[A] sprawling novel of passion and revenge. Highly recommended…It's been almost thirty years since the heyday of giant epics in the grand tradition of Edna Ferber and Barbara Taylor Bradford, but Meacham's debut might bring them back."

—*Library Journal* (starred review)

"A high-end *Thorn Birds*."

—TheDailyBeast.com

"I ate this multigenerational tale of two families warring it up across Texas history with the same alacrity with which I would gobble chocolate."

—Joshilyn Jackson, *New York Times* bestselling author of *gods in Alabama* and *Backseat Saints*

"A Southern epic in the most cinematic sense—plot-heavy and historical, filled with archaic Southern dialect and formality, with love, marriage, war, and death over three generations."

—Caroline Dworin, "The Book Bench," NewYorker.com

"This sweeping epic of love, sacrifice, and struggle reads like *Gone with the Wind* with all the passions and family politics of the South."

—*Midwest Book Review*

"The kind of book you can lose yourself in, from beginning to end."

—*Huffington Post*

"Fast-paced and full of passions...This panoramic drama proves evocative and lush. The plot is intricate and gives back as much as the reader can take...Stunning and original, *Roses* is a must-read." —TheReviewBroads.com

"May herald the overdue return of those delicious doorstop epics from such writers as Barbara Taylor Bradford and Colleen McCullough...a refreshingly nostalgic bouquet of family angst, undying love, and 'if only's." —*Publishers Weekly*

"Superbly written...a rating of ten out of ten. I simply loved this book." —*A Novel Menagerie*

CROWNING DESIGN

Leila Meacham

GC

GRAND CENTRAL
PUBLISHING

NEW YORK   BOSTON

Grand Central Publishing
Hachette Book Group
1290 Avenue of the Americas
New York, NY 10104
grandcentralpublishing.com
twitter.com/grandcentralpub

Originally published in hardcover in 1984 by the Walker Publishing Company, Inc., New York, New York.

First Grand Central Publishing Edition: January 2017

Grand Central Publishing is a division of Hachette Book Group, Inc.
The Grand Central Publishing name and logo is a trademark of Hachette Book Group, Inc.

The publisher is not responsible for websites (or their content) that are not owned by the publisher.

The Hachette Speakers Bureau provides a wide range of authors for speaking events. To find out more, go to www.hachettespeakersbureau.com or call (866) 376-6591.

Library of Congress Control Number: 2016942113.

ISBNs: 978-1-4555-4139-3 (trade pbk.), 978-1-4555-4141-6 (library edition hardcover), 978-1-4555-4138-6 (ebook)

Printed in the United States of America

LSC-C

10 9 8 7 6 5 4 3 2 1

To Richard, again

A Letter to My Friends, Fans, Readers of My Later-In-Life Novels, and Newcomers to the Books of Leila Meacham

Dear Ones,

Crowning Design *is the last to be republished of the three romances I wrote in the mid-eighties. The other two—*Ryan's Hand *and* Aly's House—*were rereleased last year with prefaces, like this one, explaining that at the time of their writing thirty-three years ago I had no idea how to go about putting together a book, a deficit that I hope will not be too apparent in this one. For those of you who have never written a book-length narrative and for those of you who would like to, let me say that there is no agony like facing a blank page in a typewriter (or computer if you are of the electronically literate) with no idea of what or who to write about when you've been paid to do so by a certain deadline. And that's exactly the position I found myself in when I first began to write* Crowning Design. Ryan's Hand *had been published, and I was under contract to produce two more romances, never having believed I could write the first one. So there I sat racking my brain to come up with* something *containing characters, plot, and setting. If I failed, I could see my advance flying from my hand back to the publisher and my name forever shamed in publishing circles.*

Now I chuckle at the huge and absurd importance I gave

myself. My advance would hardly have covered the bill for hamburgers and fries for two at a coffee shop, and nobody in "publishing circles" had a clue or cared the slightest who I was.

But I cared and I wanted to tell an interesting story. Now those of you who've read my previous letters to fans and readers as introductions to Ryan's Hand *and* Aly's House *already know that I don't follow the tried-and-true rule of fiction writing that instructs writers to write what they know. I write about what I* don't *know and then learn from research. So there I sat empty-brained the day the idea hit me for* Crowning Design. *Funny, odd, strange how a long-ago memory of a detail can leap out of the past at just the right moment and spawn a whole world (or book) of possibilities. Perhaps it only happens to writers under deadline looking at a blank page, but it happened to me. Somehow I was back in high school sitting in Miss Harbin's biology class (we called unmarried women Miss in those days), eraser in hand bearing down hard on a pituitary gland I'd drawn in the wrong place on my rendering of the human anatomy. (No mistakes were allowed.) A classmate leaned over to me. "You are rubbing too hard. If you will erase lightly, the pencil marks will disappear entirely," he said. And so I did and learned a valuable lesson that day. Better results can be achieved with gentle handling over hard pressure just about any time. But I digress. Ever afterward that school year, I followed my classmate's advice, and Miss Harbin never knew my pencil lead had landed where it shouldn't have been.*

So there it was, the one detail that would set up the mystery of who done it in Crowning Design. *After that, the other elements of fiction came fairly quickly. I would set my story in a place I'd once visited briefly but didn't know much about and would like to learn more. So Colorado it was. The Rock-*

ies, the clear mountain streams and rivers and lakes, the blue columbines, the seasons! *(We don't have seasons in Texas. Not predictable ones, anyway.) What a background against which to spin a tale! Architecture was a subject I'd wanted to know more about, so I jotted that down as a possible launchpad, and then the green light flashed. I was off and shooting forward to formulate the suspense story of* Crowning Design. *To see how those pencil marks fit into the novel, you'll have to read the book, but since you wouldn't be reading this if you did not have one in hand, I'll wish you enjoyable reading with hope this finds you well.*

Leila Meacham

CROWNING
DESIGN

Chapter One

Roger Lawson might have known his mother would get the better of him. She usually did. Why couldn't she have kept his engagement party small and simple, as he had asked—no, *ordered*—when he left for his stock-buying trip to Australia? He should have expected that in his absence she would orchestrate a bash like this and invite the entire Virginia gentry, not one of whom, by the looks of it, had declined.

Only Estelle Lawson could come up with this rose-tinted monstrosity, he fumed, looking up at the chandeliers swathed in pink net. Their twinkling lights, pink for good measure, cast a blush over everything, as if anything else was needed to give guests the illusion that they had walked into a rosy dream world. In addition to the fountain of pink champagne and musicians in pink dinner jackets, lavish arrangements of azaleas, in shades from palest blush to deepest fuchsia, were everywhere. They adorned the pink linen-draped tables, hung in heavy garlands from the balustrades, twined profusely around every column in the colonial ballroom. "To honor our Georgia beauty," Estelle explained ebulliently, wafting among her guests in a swirl of frothy chiffon the color of strawberry ice cream.

Only his mother could have pulled this off, Roger was

thinking. Only she would have wanted to. Sheer extravagance guaranteed that the Lawsonville Country Club would never again see the likes of such a party. Too much wasn't enough for her. Well, it was more than enough for him.

"It's suffocating in here," he moaned. "I feel like I'm being buried alive in cotton candy."

Deborah glanced with humor at her fiancé, a stockily built man of unexpected grace on the dance floor, and suggested, "Then let's go out to the terrace, Roger."

"With pleasure," he agreed, adroitly waltzing her to the French doors that offered escape from the flower-bedecked ballroom. "Dammit!" he said when the doors were closed behind them. "If anyone but my mother were responsible for this...but what can you do to your own mother?"

"Nothing," Deborah answered, understanding his frustration well. "No more than I can do to mine."

"Sorry you've gotten involved in all of this?"

Her laughter was the loveliest sound he'd ever heard, allaying, somewhat, his fear that she would change her mind about marrying him. "You may be the one who's sorry," she had teased.

"Never," he vowed, drawing her close. God, she was beautiful. He had never seen anyone as exquisite, as exciting, as this women he had just announced he was to marry. For once his mother and her infernal meddling in his life had paid off. That trip to Georgia last Christmas she had finagled him into taking her on... "I want to see Isabelle, Roger, and I cannot go alone. The girls are busy with their husbands' families for Christmas. It will be just the two of us this year, and why stay home when we can bask in the land of peaches and sunshine for the holidays? I want to see Isabelle. Something tells me I should. After all, I'm seventy now and there aren't many of us Kappas left from the class of '35. Look here," she had said, wagging a letter in front of him at which he barely glanced.

It had been a letter from her old sorority chum inviting them to spend Christmas in Georgia. He didn't like Georgia. It was humid and sultry even in winter, especially on the coast where the Standridges lived. He remembered the humidity from the one childhood visit he had paid with his widowed mother to the Standridges. Mr. and Mrs. Standridge had seemed old to him then, and he had thought it peculiar that they should have a five-year-old daughter. He had been fourteen then and aware that his mother was not as young as those of his friends.

The child had been a bewitching little girl, very proper and polite. She didn't whine and pull at him like pesky younger sisters of his friends. He had felt rather sorry for her, for even then he had sensed that as an only child of parents already in their fifties—a very beautiful, doll-like child—she was not being permitted a normal childhood. This perception had been verified when, bored and waiting to go into Savannah with his mother and the Standridges for dinner, he had wandered into the kitchen in search of an apple. There in the center of the room had sat the little girl on a stool as if glued to it, her eyes fixed on him when he swung open the door from the dining room.

"What are you doing?" he had demanded.

"I am to sit here after I am dressed so that I won't get mussed."

"Oh," he had said, taking in the fine lace dress with its satin sash, the black patent shoes and spotless white socks.

"How long do you have to sit there?"

"Until my parents are dressed and ready to leave."

"Is that very long?"

She had shrugged delicate shoulders, her amber eyes large and liquid in the fine-boned face.

"Do you want an apple?"

There was a basket of them, large and enticingly red. He had refused one earlier, asking if he might save it for later.

"Thank you, no. I would just get juice all over me."

"I can't imagine you ever getting anything on you."

"But I would, you see, so I can't have one."

Roger had taken an apple. It would be hours before they actually had dinner. He took it outside to eat, not caring if the succulent juice dribbled on his navy blue blazer. He sat on the stoop and thought about the little girl sitting on the stool alone in the kitchen so that she would be picture perfect when time came to show her off.

They're cruel to do that to her, he thought with disgust, thinking of his two rambunctious older sisters who had always come and gone as they pleased. They would never have allowed themselves to be planted on a kitchen stool.

That had been sixteen years ago, and now here she was, as picture perfect at twenty-one as she had been then. The body of the little girl was gone. He held the figure of a desirable woman in his arms, but the naivete and innocence were still there. In many ways, she was still the little girl sitting on the kitchen stool.

"Would you like an apple?" Roger asked.

"What?"

"An apple. Would you like to go to my place and have an apple?"

She didn't remember. He could tell by the way the amber eyes searched his face. "Ah, kitten," he said, swept by a great tenderness for the woman in his arms, "have you never done anything on the spur of the moment, disobeyed your parents, let your hair down, told the devil to take the hindmost?"

"Not very often," Deborah admitted with a small smile. "Not ever, actually. Are you asking to leave the party? Is that what the apple is all about? But what will our parents say?"

"Plenty, but what the hell?" He shrugged. "They're happy. They've got us engaged. This pony show is really for them anyway. Besides, I want to see as much of my girl as I can before she has to go back to college. What do you say?"

A faint crease disturbed the porcelain-smooth brow. "Shouldn't we at least say something to them before we leave?" she worried. His arms were very strong, she realized, and he had the kind of swarthy beard growth that required a shave twice a day. Deborah supposed she would become accustomed to the bristly feel of it next to her skin, just as she would to being the wife of a famous horse breeder and the mistress of the family estate, Lawson Downs.

The idea of both still seemed farfetched to her. Each morning now she awoke thinking that the last four months since Christmas had been a dream. As she had come down the stairs to greet Roger and his mother in the hall, she would never have had the faintest inkling that their visit would lead to this prenuptial extravaganza tonight.

Roger kissed the sweetly curving mouth. "If you say so, kitten. But the rest of the night is mine, and I don't intend to share it with that champagne-sipping crowd in there."

They found the elderly trio—Estelle Lawson, Benjamin and Isabelle Standridge—at the fountain of champagne, engaged in a private toast of their own. "Oh, there you are, my dears!" trilled Estelle, greeting them with what Roger recognized as gloating triumph. "Cheer up, Roger. I know you wanted a smaller party, but I may not have the opportunity to enjoy many more occasions like this. I was right to indulge myself, wasn't I, Deborah?"

5

Estelle's eyes were like those of a bird, Deborah thought. They were perfectly round with the yellow irises dominated by hard, black pupils. "It's a lovely party, Mrs. Lawson. Everyone seems to be having a splendid time."

"You have your mother's diplomacy, my dear. But *Mrs. Lawson* seems so formal. It won't be long before you'll be calling me Mother Lawson. You wouldn't object to that, would you, Isabelle?—Deborah calling me *Mother?*" She fastened the bird-like gaze on the woman she had known for half a century.

"Of course not," Isabelle replied, still an amazingly pretty woman, although wide swaths of silver now concealed much of the rich auburn hair Deborah had inherited. "Deborah's name for me has always been *Mummy.*"

"Oh, not always, dear," Ben hastened to contradict. "I believe she has called you *Mother* for the past several years. It sounds a little more grown-up, you know," he explained to Roger. "*Mom* might be a nice choice for you, Estelle."

"*Mom Lawson* sounds like the name of a woman running a gang of outlaws," Estelle protested. "I much prefer *Mother.*"

"Well, then," Isabelle sighed, "I guess she can still call me Mummy."

Two embarrassed spots of color had appeared on Deborah's cheeks. She turned to her fiancé decisively. "Roger, did you say something about an apple?"

Roger grinned. "That I did. If you folks will excuse us, we're going to the kitchen for an apple. Don't wait up." Seeing his mother about to protest, he gripped Deborah's elbow and steered her toward the ballroom doors before the trio could organize their objections.

"They've finally gotten to you, haven't they?" Roger commented as he drove out of the club parking lot in the direction of his condominium overlooking the Potomac River.

Deborah pressed her throbbing temples. The headache had been with her for the entire round of exhausting prenuptial activities. "I am so weary of that kind of discussion. Would it ever occur to either of our mothers to ask *me* what I might like to call your mother?"

Roger found that observation amusing. "When we're married," he chuckled, "you'll have your say in everything. I guarantee it."

Deborah did not respond. How grand it would be, she sighed inwardly, if Roger did not have to shield her from the domination of his mother. She'd had enough of that from her own parents. Now she wondered if she weren't, by marrying into Roger's formidable family, just adding another thumb to the two she'd lived under all her short life. Estelle Lawson was one of those matriarchs who had reared two daughters and a son to knuckle under to no one, not even to her, and Deborah instinctively knew that had they done so, offspring or not, Estelle would have ground them under her heel. Deborah had never bucked anyone or any decision made for her in her life. What chance would she have to lead her own life in a house with such a woman? For it was understood that while Deborah would assume the title and duties of mistress of Lawson Downs, her mother-in-law would continue to occupy a wing of the mansion.

"You're thinking mighty hard over there, kitten. What's going on in that lovely head of yours? Not reconsidering marrying me, are you?" It was a fear that he could not lay to rest. He knew that the decision to marry him had not been hers. Accustomed from infancy to accepting what her parents thought best for her, Deborah had yet to realize that she could make decisions for herself. The little show of assertiveness awhile ago had delighted him, but she must not be encouraged to try her wings too often—not until they were married. Once discovered, she just might fly away from them all.

"Tell me you're happy," he said.

"Roger, of course I'm happy. How could I not be? You're the catch of every girl's dream. Just ask my sorority sisters!" She laughed and described how her roommates had been green with envy after one of his visits to Georgia Tech.

"But am I the catch of *your* dreams, Deborah?" he asked, reaching for her hand while he steered the Mercedes through the Saturday evening traffic.

The question caught Deborah off guard. She did not allow herself dreams. They too often conflicted with those of her parents. Once she had secretly hoped to become a famous building designer, maybe even the leader in a new concept of architectural design. But she had always known that the architectural degree she was working so diligently to earn was only a pastime until marriage. Her parents were getting on in years. They had made it clear that they must have the peace of knowing that responsibility for their only child's security had been transferred to a loving husband. Hope had been voiced that there might even be a grandchild or two to sweeten the ravages of age.

Glancing at the swarthy figure behind the wheel, Deborah answered honestly, "Not only of mine, Roger, but of my parents. You are as ideal a husband as they could wish for me."

Roger longed to ask the next question but contented himself with her affectionate squeeze of his thumb.

At his condominium, a bachelor retreat he maintained as a haven from the all-seeing eyes of his mother, Roger picked up an envelope from several that lay on the carpet beneath the mail slot. Opening it quickly, he scanned the contents and hooted delightedly. "Good ol' Bear! I knew he wouldn't let me down!"

"Bear?"

"My best man. We grew up together. We're like brothers. He's in South America now, constructing buildings for an oil company. I didn't know until now if he would be able to make it to the wedding. Make yourself at home, kitten, while I read this. You don't mind, do you? It's been awhile since I've heard from him."

"No, go ahead. I'll just get acquainted with your friends here," Deborah said, indicating the stuffed animal heads arranged around the walls. *Bear.* The name suggested something huge and hairy, like the heads of these hapless creatures. She hoped that Roger, by evidence an avid hunter, did not expect her to take up the sport. She adored animals. The idea of shooting one was abhorrent to her.

Roger finished the letter, smiling to himself, and shed the white dinner jacket and black tie. "You'll like Bear," he said, going to the bar built into the wall. "He says he won't believe you until he sees you, that no girl could be the paragon I've described."

Deborah, watching him work with seltzer bottle and ice, was not listening. She was watching his small hands, realizing that they were disproportionate to the rest of his strong, stocky body. Black, wiry hair sprang from the backs of them, and the nails were rather long. Soon they would have access to her body. The thought of that eventuality compressed the air from her lungs in a seizure of panic. What was she doing sitting in this oppressively masculine room beneath the sightless eyes of animals killed to decorate the walls? Deborah's head throbbed. She had to stifle an hysterical impulse to flee the room and the swarthy stranger coming forward with a tray of drinks.

"Here we are, a couple of fine apples," Roger said, setting down the tray of drinks. Handing Deborah a glass, his rib cage contracted at the look on her face. "Deborah—kitten! What is it?"

With a strained smile, Deborah asked testily, "Roger, would you mind not calling me kitten? It makes me sound so—so insubstantial. And I'm not, you know. Everybody seems to have forgotten that I am about to graduate *cum laude* with a degree in architectural design. I can assure you that I wouldn't be if I were in the least...kitten-like."

Roger regarded her without speaking, still feeling the spasm in his midsection. After a moment, he said in tender understanding, "You're scared, aren't you?"

Deborah dropped her gaze. "I just can't understand why you would want to marry me. I know you say you love me, but I don't understand that either. You're older and sophisticated and worldly. I know nothing about horses or hunting or running a home like Lawson Downs. I don't know anything about—about—" She blushed as her tongue wrapped around the word.

"About sex?" Roger asked. "Don't you think I know that, Deborah? That is one of the reasons I find you so appealing. Don't worry about being inexperienced—in anything. I'm a patient man, and I will never rush you into anything you don't want—after we're married," he added smoothly, hoping she hadn't noticed the correction. "I promise you that. You'll enjoy being my wife. You'll enjoy the estate and the little town of Lawsonville. The community will love you. You'll blossom, Deborah. You'll be free. No more kitchen stools for you!"

Deborah lifted her eyes in wonder, slowly recollecting the time, long ago in Savannah, when Roger had found her on a stool in the kitchen. He had come looking for an apple. "Roger!" she cried in full understanding. "Now I remember! Now I know what you meant by that question about the apple!" Laughing, she looked at him with affection. He was so kind and good. She was just tired, that was all, and sick from the headache.

But it was with relief when several days later Deborah let herself into the suite she shared with two sorority sisters on the campus of the Georgia Institute of Technology. The girls were in class. A note laying on the desk read: *Deborah, call Dr. Corbet. Important.*

Puzzled, Deborah dialed the number scrawled on the note, wondering why the chairman of her graduate committee had called. She had already met with him for their last advisory session before finals.

"Deborah, my girl, I realize you have plans to marry soon after graduation," said Dr. Corbet when he came on the line, "but I think you should know that Randall Hayden called me from Denver a few days ago to inquire about you."

"*The* Randall Hayden?" Deborah inquired, referring to the renowned architect who had critiqued her thesis project. She had never met him.

"He wants to interview you for a job."

Dr. Corbet said no more, allowing time for that information to sink in. He had been deeply disappointed when informed that his most gifted student would not be pursuing an architectural career. "Did you tell him that I am to be married a week after graduation?" Deborah asked.

"No-o-o," drawled Dr. Corbet. "I thought I'd let you do that. Here's his number. Why don't you give him a call?"

Deborah glanced at her watch. It would be ten o'clock in Denver, probably a good time for reaching the founder of a firm that had helped to launch the postmodern movement in building design. She was enormously flattered by his interest. "The least I can do," Deborah said, "is thank him for thinking of me."

"My thoughts exactly," said Dr. Corbet.

A pleasant-voiced secretary put her through immediately to Randall Hayden. "Why, Miss Standridge, how good to hear from you," he said warmly. "When can you come to Denver for an interview? We are interviewing designers for a position in our urban planning department."

"I am honored to be considered, Mr. Hayden."

"Then you'll come? Shall we say the day after tomorrow? Call Mrs. Talbert back when you've made your flight reservations, and we'll schedule the appointment according to your arrival time. She'll also give you directions to our offices. The firm, of course, will bear all expenses. We'll be seeing you Wednesday then?"

"Yes," said Deborah breathlessly, staring down at the telephone base as though she'd never seen it before.

"Good. I look forward to meeting you."

Deborah hung up in amazement. What in the world had come over her? She must call Mrs. Talbert back immediately and apologize, saying that she couldn't possibly go to Denver for an interview. She must explain that somehow, during the moments of talking with Mr. Hayden, everything but the chance to work for him had simply flown from her mind. She had forgotten that in a month's time she was to be married.

Deborah did not call Mrs. Talbert back. Ignoring the promptings of both conscience and reason, she spent the next forty minutes arranging a morning flight to Denver. When next she spoke with Mrs. Talbert, it was to tell the secretary of her arrival time. Her interview with Mr. Hayden was scheduled accordingly.

Wednesday morning, Deborah lingered behind after her roommates went down to breakfast and hurriedly packed a bag, leaving a note saying she would be back tomorrow. The girls knew that Deborah had been morose lately—"the bridal jitters," they called it. They would think she merely wanted to be alone for a while.

An hour later, fastening her seat belt, Deborah remembered Roger's words: "Have you never done anything on the spur of the moment...never told the devil to take the hindmost?" For once in her life she was doing exactly that. The experience was exhilarating. She almost laughed aloud as the plane lifted off.

Denver had long fascinated her. She had never been there, but she had read about its robust lifestyle and climate, its lusty gold-mining origins so unlike the genteel traditions of Savannah. Having grown up near a sultry seacoast, she had often thought how refreshing it would be to live in a city bounded by mountains glistening with snow even in summer.

As the plane descended, she sat with her nose pressed to the window, captivated by the mountain peaks topped with snow, brilliant against the blue sky. In the taxi she rolled down the windows and breathed in the fresh, invigorating air. Denver had problems with smog, she had read, but not today. It was the end of May, and there was still an icicle clarity about the atmosphere. Savannah was already sweltering under unprecedented heat.

"Miss Standridge, it is a pleasure to meet you," Randall Hayden said, laying aside his pipe and rising at her entrance. "I hope we didn't take you away from end-of-year exams?"

"Not at all, Mr. Hayden," Deborah said, taking the slender hand and smiling into the gentle eyes. "Finals begin next week."

"From what Dr. Corbet says, I've every reason to believe they will present no problem."

"I hope you're right," she said, warming to the kindly voice and courtly manner. She thought he must be in his early sixties—a slightly built, somewhat stooped gentleman with an old-fashioned, gracious air about him. He wore a bow tie and a vest with a watch chain. His fair hair and brows were going white, and his eyes were the blue of a mild summer sky. He was like his buildings, Deborah decided—a tasteful blend of modernism tempered with the quiet elegance of a bygone age.

"We must repair our inner cities, Miss Standridge," Randall gravely explained on a tour of his offices an hour later. "If we do not, they will disintegrate into ghettos. We architects and those affiliated with our enterprises must turn our attention from suburbia, from the shopping malls and condominiums, and begin concentrating on making our downtowns liveable once again. The Hayden firm is committing itself to urban renewal. That is why we are expanding our urban planning department."

Deborah, listening intently, wondered what it would be like to work for this man. "This is the office, just completed, that the newest member of our firm will occupy," said Randall, opening a door whose brass nameplate was as yet unengraved. Deborah stepped inside. The smell peculiar to newly constructed rooms greeted her. There was no furniture, but her feet sank into plush pale blue carpet. A bay window looked out onto a patch of ground laid out for landscaping. There, in front of the window, should go a curved desk, definitely cherry she decided, and imagined heavy chintz draperies in light blue and cream. Randall said nothing, but puffed his pipe and observed.

"Well!" said Deborah brightly. "Your firm certainly does well by its newcomers."

"We try," Randall said mildly.

On the return flight, Deborah consoled herself with the certain conviction that someone of her total inexperience would never be offered the job anyway. It was enough to have been exposed, even briefly, to the creative, busy atmosphere of the Hayden firm and to have met its venerable founder. She had satisfied her impulse. Now she must get back to Georgia, study for finals, and prepare for the wedding. Mr. Hayden had promised to notify her of the firm's decision, one way or the other.

That weekend Roger came to the campus for a last visit until the week of the wedding. She had finals, and he had several stock-buying trips abroad that he wanted out of the way before they went on their honeymoon. "But I am going to miss you," Roger breathed huskily as he held her the last night before returning to Virginia.

"I'll miss you, too," Deborah said dutifully, "but it's only three weeks until we see each other again." They were parked in the Mercedes, and Roger was nuzzling her neck. "Roger..." Deborah murmured, pressing his head close to her throat. She wanted so much to feel something. She had to feel something. She *must* feel something! His lips and breath hot on her bare skin, Deborah could have screamed from disappointment.

Recently, in a worried moment, her mother had confided that she had not loved Deborah's father when they were first married. "But I came to love him, darling," she had said encouragingly, stroking her daughter's hair back from a face that had shown too much strain lately. "And we've had a wonderfully...satisfying marriage, like the kind you'll have with Roger. Truly, dear."

Now, in desperation, Deborah willed herself to respond to Roger, but it was no use. Perhaps after the wedding...Her parents were still devoted to each other, even at their ages. Roger, feeling her tension, held her gently. "It's going to be wonderful, honey. I promise," he said.

Three weeks later, Deborah was dressing for her final bridal luncheon when the call came from Denver. "It's long distance, darling," her mother called up the stairs just as the doorbell

15

rang. Through the door's glass insets, Deborah could see the uniformed mailman with another load of wedding packages.

"I'll take it up here, Mother," she said from the landing, picking up the receiver. "This is Deborah Standridge."

"Miss Standridge, Randall Hayden here! How are you, my dear?"

Nearly married, Deborah felt like responding, but she replied, "Well, thank you. And you?"

"Happy, Miss Standridge, very happy indeed. I speak on behalf of the entire firm when I say that we are most eager for you to come join our urban planning department." Randall chuckled in understanding when Deborah did not reply for a few seconds. "Um, Miss Standridge, are you still there?"

"Mr. Hayden, I—I never expected to be hired. I—I don't know what to say—"

"*Yes* would be sufficient, my dear. However, if you wish to be verbose, you might try, 'Yes, I would love to come work for your firm.' Shall I repeat that?" Laughter laced his words.

"No, that won't be necessary. Yes, I would love to come work for your firm."

"Splendid! Now I realize you've just graduated, and you need a couple of weeks to rest and get organized, not to mention finding a place to live in Denver. Shall we say your employment begins two weeks from today? If you need an advance on your salary—"

"No, I can manage. Thank you, Mr. Hayden. You'll see me in two weeks."

"Oh, Miss Standridge, before you hang up—we're in the process of landscaping the ground outside the bay window of your office. What kind of tree would you prefer for it?"

"An aspen. I'd like an aspen tree, Mr. Hayden," Deborah replied.

Deborah was thoughtfully replacing the phone as her mother came to the foot of the stairs, the smile she had used for the mailman still in place. She was wearing peach linen, one of the bridal colors. Deborah was in yellow. Isabelle looked up at the strange set of her daughter's face. "Who was that, dear?"

"Randall Hayden. He's the president of the Hayden architectural firm of Denver. He offered me a job. I accepted."

The smile slipped from Isabelle's face. "You did what?"

Slowly, Deborah came down the stairs. Her eyes were pleading. "Mother, I can't marry Roger. I don't love him. He is a wonderful man, but he's not for me. I don't want to get married. I never did. I just wanted to make you and Daddy happy."

Although Isabelle had never appeared her age, she now looked every one of her seventy years. "You don't mean that, darling. You're just tired. Finals and then all of these back-to-back activities have taken a lot out of you. What you're experiencing is commonly known as cold feet, a typical bridal syndrome. You'll get over it. Now finish dressing. We're late."

"Mother, you didn't hear me. I am not going to the luncheon. I am not marrying Roger. I am going to Denver to work as an urban designer for the Hayden architectural firm."

Isabelle looked around wildly, as if searching for reinforcements. "Ben!" she yelled. "Your father will have something to say about this, young lady. This is absurd. You're making us late for the luncheon. Ben!"

Deborah followed her mother outside to the garden, where they found Benjamin Standridge contemplating a bed of snapdragons. He was suffering his usual yearly qualms about having to behead the central stems in order to force the plants to bush out and make new blossoms. "Yes, dears, what is it?" he addressed the two colorful blurs occupying his side vision and began his pruning.

Both women spoke at once, one in anger, the other in appeal. Ultimately, each jumbled entreaty registered. "What is this, Deborah?" Ben said, getting to his feet. "You say you don't want to marry Roger? But why on earth not?"

"I don't love him, Daddy. I—"

"What has that got to do with anything!" Isabelle snapped. "I told you how it would be!" Ben blinked at his wife in bewilderment, not quite sure that he was grasping everything. "Say something, Ben!" Isabelle ordered.

Jerkily, Ben complied. "Every bride, indeed every groom, goes through these last-minute doubts about the person they've chosen to marry," he counseled. "It's quite normal."

"Daddy, I am not marrying Roger. I have to call him right now. He's chartered a plane for his part of the wedding party. I have to call him so that he can tell them all the wedding is off."

Isabelle began to cry. Benjamin stared in shock. "Deborah, dear, but you can't do this…"

"Daddy, I have to. Please try to understand and forgive me. I can't marry Roger just to please you and Mother. Our marriage would be a terrible mistake, more so for Roger than for me. I am so sorry about all of this, but isn't it better to know now than find out later?" Her parents remained speechless. "I—I must telephone," Deborah said. "Don't you see I must call before all of those people begin arriving at Lawson Downs?"

Still they stared, the shock giving way to silent condemnation. Deborah gave each of them a kiss on the cheek. Her mother's was wet with tears. "I'm so sorry, Mother," she said and left her parents in the garden.

Roger was overjoyed at hearing Deborah's voice. She had finally located him in a roadside hangout where his stockmen had taken him for an impromptu bachelor party. "Speak a little louder, honey," he yelled into the phone, shouting over a background din of boisterous voices and loud jukebox music. Deborah had to hold the receiver away from her ear. "There's quite a racket in this place. What is so urgent that you had to call me here?"

Deborah told him. She had wanted so much to be gentle, but the noise made it necessary to yell. "I'll call you back!" Roger shouted at last. "Don't leave the phone. I'll call you back in a few minutes."

While she waited in an agony of remorse, Deborah could hear her mother sobbing and Benjamin offering broken words of consolation. Roger was not shouting when she answered his ring. "I'm in the owner's office," he explained, and Deborah could hear his struggle to remain calm. "Now go over all of that again."

Gently, Deborah obeyed, her heart breaking for his grief and disappointment. When she had finished, he said in a voice shattered with despair, "Deborah, don't do this. Please don't."

"Roger, my dear, I care too much for you not to—" The line suddenly went dead.

For two days, without assistance from Isabelle, Deborah canceled the wedding preparations. She wrote letters of apology to Roger and Estelle, returned and readdressed packages to their senders, and answered the constant stream of telephone calls with determination. Isabelle shut herself in her room, refusing to speak to Deborah, and Benjamin remained in his study. On the evening of the second day, he answered the phone on his desk. Deborah was in the kitchen heating soup to entice her mother to eat.

Ben came to stare at Deborah from the doorway of the kitchen, his mouth working strangely. "Daddy, what is the matter?"

"You'd better pick up the phone in here," he said with difficulty. "Estelle Lawson is on the line."

Deborah braced herself and lifted the receiver. "Yes, Mrs. Lawson?" she said quietly.

"I just thought you ought to know, Deborah," came the cold, precise intonation, "that for the rest of my life I will hold you responsible for the death of my son."

Chapter Two

Deborah stood at the bay window, looking out at the aspen leaves flickering and flashing in the September sunshine. They had always reminded her of a mass meeting of butterflies, even when the tree had been a skimpy sapling eight years ago. That fall all but three of the "butterflies" had flown away. The three that remained had turned a bright red and had hung on through the fall months like nervous survivors of a long battle.

Deborah had watched from the window as finally, one after the other, they had drifted to the ground in the blustery winter days. She had felt a chilled sense of loss. The desiccated leaves had made her think of the three elderly friends who had once drunk champagne together beneath the rosy lights of chandeliers. They, too, in the succeeding winters, their grips on life broken, had followed one another in death.

She tensed when the knock came at the door and left the window to slip several sketches into a portfolio lying on the orderly desk. "Come in," she called.

The door opened, and Bea Talbert entered. She said after a brief, compassionate silence, "They're ready for you, Deborah."

Deborah smiled wryly. "You say that as if I'm being summoned to hear my sentence. So the jury is in place, is it? Any idea of the verdict?"

"Sorry. Can't help you there. How do you feel?"

"Scared. I don't want to lose this one, Bea."

"You won't, sweetie pie. Now come here and let's have a look at you."

Deborah walked around the curved cherry desk and submitted herself to the critical eye of a woman whose maternal regard she had enjoyed throughout the last eight years.

"You look sensational," Bea pronounced, fluffing at the bow of Deborah's silk blouse. "That suit becomes you. You don't have a thing to worry about. Once those men get a look at you, they won't be able to deny you anything."

"How I wish you were right, Bea. But I've learned that when it comes to businessmen, nothing can compete with the bottom line. What I'm counting on is the strength of those designs winning us this bid." Deborah tucked the portfolio under her arm and followed Bea out. Together they walked down the corridor to the conference room.

"What's the weather like in there?" she asked.

"Stormy the couple of times I've been in. The men were discussing the fate of your friends' establishments. They were all talking at once, and Randall had to rap for order."

"Oh, goodness. Well, were they for keeping them or razing them?"

"Honestly, Deborah, I couldn't tell. The pros and cons sounded evenly divided to me."

"What did Daniel Parker have to say?"

"Nothing. Just sat back and listened. He keeps his own counsel, that one. The others seem to treat him deferentially. I'd say that if you can sell that big fellow, you've sold the others."

"That's what I think, too. What's he like?"

Bea sighed. "The kind of man who makes me wish I were twenty years younger. You don't see many of his kind anymore.

He's not a handsome man, just very striking and—dynamic. It should be interesting when you two meet."

"Bea, you're an incurable romantic. I was asking about his temperament, not his looks. And you can forget about any fireworks between us. Daniel Parker will have his mind on one thing only in there today—business."

She was certain of that. Deborah always researched the background of potential clients before designing a building as part of a Hayden bid. Research on Daniel Parker had revealed that the man lived and breathed only for making money. He was both a developer and a builder, having started his own company almost before he had graduated from college. Although she had uncovered little about his origins, he had apparently grown up in poverty. She had learned little else about him except that at thirty-eight he was still a bachelor and an addicted jogger. This last information had inspired her to include an indoor running track on the top floor of the building she had designed for his corporate headquarters when he moved his business from Phoenix to Denver.

The problem today had arisen when the Parker Corporation purchased a block of Cutter Street as the site for its headquarters in a proposed business complex. Learning of the sale, Deborah had gone immediately to Randall to ask if the firm might submit a bid for the project. He had been surprised and asked why, saying that the firm already had more business than it could handle, Deborah in particular.

Because, she had explained, Josie's Bar and Fred's Paper Shack sat juxtaposed in the center of the block. The buildings were leased by two colorful downtown characters who had become good friends of hers, and if another firm got the contract, their places of business could be razed right out from under them. Couldn't she at least sketch a preliminary workup of the area to show how the business complex could be designed around the two structures, thus allowing them to stand?

Well, as Tony Pierson often said, "Whatever Deborah asks, that she shall receive." Randall had approved her reasons and had praised the sketches. The firm had drawn up a mortgage package and had submitted a bid for the project. She was being summoned now to defend retaining the two little businesses when neither had shown much profit for years.

"Well, here we are," Bea said cheerfully as they approached the wide double doors of the conference room. "Are you ready?"

"As ready as I'll ever be," Deborah replied, taking a deep breath between the hammer beats of her heart.

"Then let's go get 'em, tiger!"

It was the moment for which Randall Hayden had been waiting all morning. He was not to be disappointed. Bea Talbert, his trusted secretary for twenty-five years, had an appreciation for the dramatic and a sense of timing that seldom erred. All heads turned as the double doors opened. Bea, assuming her haughtiest pose, stood momentarily in the doorway, her large elegant figure blocking from view the young woman behind her. "Gentlemen," she announced coolly, "Deborah Standridge," and stepped aside to leave Deborah framed in the doorway.

Perfect! thought Randall, clamping down hard on his pipe to keep from smiling. He never failed to be entertained by the reactions of other men to Deborah's beauty. She had a marvelous face and figure, her poise and carriage giving an illusion of greater height than she possessed. All but one of the five men were rising quickly to their feet, squaring shoulders and adjusting coats. Dan Parker rose slowly, almost reluctantly.

His reaction—or lack of it—puzzled Randall. The strongly

carved features, the level blue eyes, revealed nothing but merely retained the inscrutable reserve with which he had earlier greeted the storm of protest arising over one aspect of the mortgage package. "Let's wait and hear out the architect," had been his comment. The others had taken it as an admonition and gone to other matters. Now Randall, observing his stony regard of Deborah, felt a cold apprehension. He went to her quickly and placed a protective arm about her shoulders. With the pride of a father, he made the introductions. He left until last the presentation of his protégé to Dan Parker.

There was a moment of silence as the two extraordinary people shook hands. "Miss Standridge," the builder acknowledged simply, his deeply modulated voice a proper accompaniment to his impressive size. "You've put together quite a package. Mind answering a few questions about it?"

"That is why I am here," she answered a bit stiffly, at once judging him to be the kind of man who would rebuff an attempt to charm. The gray hair was definitely premature, but somehow it suited him, she decided, noting the contrast with his clear blue eyes and darkly tanned skin. He had the power and presence of a mountain. Mountains were among her favorite things, but this one was discomfiting. She had the impression that she was trespassing on unfriendly territory.

Withdrawing her hand, she looked about for a chair. Clayton Thomas, introduced as a banker from New York, quickly pulled one out, smiling broadly. "Don't be afraid of us, Miss Standridge," he said urbanely. "We never eat lovely, auburn-haired young architects before lunch."

"In that case I'd better hurry to satisfy your questions before then." Deborah smiled, taking a seat.

Polite laughter, joined by all but Daniel Parker, lightened the atmosphere. At the head of the table, Randall set down his pipe and laced his long, sensitive fingers together. "The gentlemen would like to know, Deborah, why you feel it necessary to preserve Josie's Bar and Fred's Paper Shack on Cutter Street."

"You can understand our concern from a businessman's point of view, I am sure," explained Clayton Thomas smoothly. Of the group, he had been the most hotly opposed to allowing a dingy little bar and newspaper stand to remain on the site intended for an important business center. After all, it wasn't as if either of them were an historical landmark! "Josie's Bar and Fred's Paper Shack would detract from the appearance of the other buildings, not to mention the financial liability they would be to the corporation until the deaths or retirements of the tenants. As you have mentioned in your report, neither of these two tenants can afford to pay the lease once the project is completed. The corporation would have to absorb the cost of their rents. And then with the demise or retirement of these two people, we would be left with two white elephants on our hands." He gave Deborah the flash of his smile to soften any sting his words might have. She was a knockout, and he still had two evenings left in Denver before returning to New York and his third wife. She would probably welcome the opportunity of wooing his vote.

One of the other five spoke up. "Personally, I think your designs are wonderful. Beautiful as well as functional. But it seems absurd to me that you would want to build them around those two straggly businesses."

"What the consensus here seems to be, Miss Standridge," interposed the deep voice of Dan Parker, "is that they would be costly eyesores. We're asking you to explain why they shouldn't be leveled with all the other original structures on that block."

Their eyes met. Deborah saw something in his she could not fathom. Dislike? Disdain? Perhaps he was one of those men opposed to women in business. He seemed the type. She glanced quickly at Randall before replying. He gazed back at her benignly, unperturbed. The slender fingers still lay peacefully entwined.

"Gentlemen," Deborah began quietly, addressing the group as a whole and avoiding the steady eye of Dan Parker. "Have any of you visited either place?" Their expressions affirmed that they had not. "I think you would find that Josie's Bar would never be a white elephant. It would require some renovation, certainly, when Josie Peabody retires, but the structure itself is in excellent shape. You shouldn't have any trouble leasing it as a bar. The interior alone would lure prospective tenants."

"Even with competition from the bar of the hotel we'll be building on the block?" questioned another of the five, a heavyset man with a pugnacious manner.

"A different crowd frequents Josie's," Deborah answered. "In Denver, most bars cater to occupational groups. The factory workers who have drunk beer for years in Josie's would never feel at home in a hotel cocktail lounge."

"What about Fred's Paper Shack?" asked another member of the investment group. "There we're not talking about a great deal of floor space. We'd have to knock out walls to accommodate another type of business concern."

"Not necessarily," Deborah argued patiently, happening to glance at Dan Parker as she reached for her portfolio. She realized suddenly that the man's incisive attention was not really focused on her replies but was focused on her personally. Yet there was not a trace of admiration in those clear blue eyes. What was he thinking about?

Discomfited again, she drew out a number of sketches and passed them around the table. "These are preliminary drawings of business possibilities that I feel would prosper in that space," she said. "It's an ideal location for a stationery and card stand, craft shop, boutique, or exotic foods shop. Even a small bookstore would probably do very well there."

While waiting for the men to study the drawings, Deborah cast a brief look at Randall. He gave the head of his urban planning department a quick wink and reached for his pipe.

"All right," Dan said, "you've given us the commercial arguments for retaining them. What are your personal ones?"

Deborah shifted in her seat, vexed by the blunt tone. He was indeed a profit-motivated businessman, and she wasn't winning him. "Those are harder to sell but just as important. The families of Josie Peabody and Fred Sims have occupied those two establishments since before the second World War. The businesses were legacies handed down to the present tenants. To the people who live and work in that area—I'm talking about the true city dwellers, not the suburban commuters who will be working in your buildings—Josie's Bar and Fred's Paper Shack are an integral part of their lives. A morning couldn't begin without buying a paper from Fred or end without a beer in Josie's. And those patrons represent more than just a livelihood to Josie and Fred. Since neither of them have any living relatives, they are like family to them."

Deborah paused a moment. She had been addressing her remarks around the table but now directed them to Dan. "It would be impossible for those two to relocate as the other tenants on the block have done. The bar and Josie, the paper stand and Fred, are inseparable. You might as well try to move a tree without its roots. It wouldn't survive. Neither would Josie or Fred."

"You are asking us then," said the heavyset man, "to consider the two establishments from the viewpoint of charity rather than economics."

Deborah flashed an irritated look at the speaker. "Josie and

Fred would be offended by *charity*. They've paid their dues to Denver, enough to allow them to live out their working lives in peace. *Sentiment* might be a better viewpoint from which to consider them. Sentiment and profits are not necessarily oil-and-water mixtures. They can occasionally be successfully blended."

She thought she saw the briefest glint of amusement in the blue eyes across the table before Clayton Thomas drew her attention. "And how do you propose to blend the two, my dear?" he asked, smarting a bit from the little knuckle rap she had given them as businessmen. "The fact is that this corporation would be out a considerable sum on behalf of *sentiment*, let alone the inconvenience and costs of renovation when these people do retire."

"Oh, Mr. Thomas." Deborah could feel her patience giving way. "The favorable publicity the corporation would receive from allowing that pair to remain on Cutter Street would more than offset the sacrifice of the loss in their lease money or any further costs. Tenants would be standing in line to lease space from such a humane corporation."

"How old are Josie and Fred?" inquired Dan unexpectedly.

"In their seventies."

Again their gazes locked. The dark brows arched slightly, and Deborah was subjected to a short cryptic scrutiny before Dan diverted his attention to the head of the table. Deborah felt her heart drop. She had lost the case for Fred and Josie. "Randall," Dan said, "would you care at this time to state the firm's position on this matter?"

Randall was concentrating on re-lighting his pipe. He did not reply or look at his audience until that was accomplished. Deborah held her breath. She didn't know if Randall would support her on this. She wasn't certain she wanted him to. She had come

to recognize the fact that architectural offices needed clients, profits, and growth potential for their own health and for that of their
clients. If Randall was adamant about Fred and Josie, these men
would simply take their business elsewhere. The city block and
all its buildings were theirs to raze or preserve. If this corporation
selected another firm to design its buildings, Fred and Josie
would lose anyway, and so would Randall Hayden.

"Gentlemen," began Randall, "the Hayden firm for the past
eight years has been particularly committed to urban revitaliza-
tion. Unfortunately that commitment has involved, more often
than not, the tearing down of the old to rebuild the new. But
in this case, I do not think it is necessary to destroy two viable
and beloved business concerns. The uniqueness of a city, an inner city with a heritage like Denver's, cannot survive when the
Josies and the Freds are driven out. Miss Standridge has ingeniously shown you how you can build your complex around
them, preserving their livelihoods and the familiar services they
provide. And I agree with her. As much as this firm would appreciate your business, gentlemen, if you insist on razing those
two buildings, the firm will withdraw the bid."

A silence followed, broken by the sound of Randall pushing his
chair back. He bestowed upon Deborah his mellow smile. "Thank
you for coming, Miss Standridge. We'll not detain you any longer."

Acknowledging her dismissal, Deborah closed her aston-
ished mouth and rose. Immediately, the men did likewise. She
gave the group a strained smile. "Thank you for the courtesy of
your attention," she said politely, nodding to Randall and hur-
rying out.

Back at her desk, Deborah plopped dispiritedly into the chair
and stared into space. Good Lord! She had just cost the firm
a commission worth a fortune! If only she had been less abra-
sive, more charming. If only Randall did not *believe* in her so

much! If only that Daniel Parker with his silver-gray hair and ice-blue eyes had not been so unmoved by her! *What was with him anyway?*

She bit her lip reflectively. She was unaccustomed to such indifference from men. Although she had never used her looks to win concessions in her field, she had to admit that today she would not have minded if they had influenced the discussion. So much was at stake. This one time she was not above using any advantage to win the contract and to save Josie and Fred from being turned out into the street. Well, so much for her looks!

"How did it go?" Bea demanded, poking her head around the door. Above it another one appeared. It belonged to Tony Pierson, a tall, loosely jointed young man with an engaging grin, a member of the team who had put together the mortgage package.

Deborah regarded the pair dismally. "Not so well, I regret to say. If I were a betting woman, I'd say we lost the ball game."

"And just why is that, Deborah?" demanded another voice behind Bea and Tony. Its owner, a thin, sallow-faced man in a brown suit, pushed open the door to stare accusingly at the rival occupying the seat that should have gone to him five years before. "Could it be that Randall supported your mawkish regard for Fred and Josie and refused to sell the plans if their buildings are razed?"

"You know the man well, John." Deborah sighed. "Randall did exactly that."

"I swear, Deborah—" John raked a hand through his dry, characterless brown hair. "Randall would support you if you wanted to design a skyscraper on an ice floe!"

"Hardly a comparison to Deborah's proposal," Bea scolded sternly. "You ought to be proud of her—and of Randall's stand. The Hayden firm would never be a party to the destruction of those establishments, not for any amount of money."

Ignoring the rebuke, John continued. "Just what are you trying to prove with this crusade of yours, Deborah? Somehow it doesn't fit the high society image we know."

"That *you* know," Tony contended. "The rest of us have no trouble at all in understanding Deborah's regard for Fred and Josie—"

The loud clearing of a throat behind them ended the confrontation abruptly. Deborah stood up. At the door was another visitor, the suave Clayton Thomas. He entered the room, smiling smoothly, and Deborah wondered how much of the exchange he had overheard. "I do hope I'm not interrupting anything," he said complacently.

"Of course not, Mr. Thomas," said Deborah, coming from around her desk. "May I present my colleagues, Tony Pierson, who helped to prepare the bid, and John Turner, our chief structural engineer. Mr. Hayden's secretary, Bea Talbert, I believe you know."

After an exchange of greetings, Clayton turned to Deborah. "I thought you might like to know that the decision has not been made yet. We're all to meet tomorrow morning for a final vote after a good night's sleep on the matter."

"Very sensible, I am sure," John agreed readily.

"I've a question or two to ask you, Miss Standridge, if you don't mind." Clayton said pointedly. Taking the hint, Deborah escorted the others to the door.

"See if you can salvage it, will you, love?" murmured John as he was leaving. "I'm sure you'll think of a way." She shut the door on his insinuating smile.

Turning back to Clayton and suspecting what was coming, Deborah asked, "What questions do you have?"

"One, will you have dinner with me—so that we can further discuss this business—and two, will you introduce me to Fred and Josie this evening? I don't want to cast a vote without having met them. I thought it might be enlightening to have a nightcap in Josie's Bar. How does that sound?"

"I'd like that," Deborah said without hesitation. "Except that I'm not free for dinner. I'd be happy, however, to meet you for a nightcap at Josie's. I can't promise that Fred will be there, but he usually is."

Clayton was careful to conceal his disappointment. After all, a half loaf was better than none. "Wonderful!" he exclaimed with false heartiness. "Since I'll not have the pleasure of your company for dinner, I'll dine alone at my hotel. I am at the Brown Palace. Do you think you could pick me up in the lobby at nine, and we can go to Josie's together?"

With as much grace as she could manage, Deborah agreed. "I am delighted." The financier beamed. He held out a well-manicured hand and clasped hers for a long, warm minute. "I look forward to a lengthy discussion afterward."

Deborah allowed a brief smile to suffice as a response and led him to the door. When he was gone, she sighed wearily, under no illusion as to why Clayton Thomas wanted her company this evening. Clients had exerted this kind of pressure on her before when the Hayden firm was bidding with others for the same contract. She had learned that the simplest response was to make herself unavailable. But Clayton Thomas had outmaneuvered her by asking to meet Fred and Josie. They were a ploy to have her company for the evening, of course, but there was a slim chance that the irrepressible pair just might sway his judgment in their behalf. It was worth a try.

"Oh, my dear—" breathed Clayton reverently as he took her hand in the magnificent rotunda of the Brown Palace Hotel.

"Your dinner date probably threw himself on the floor and howled after you left him tonight."

"He'll survive." Deborah smiled, amused at how close Clayton had come in describing Dempsey's reaction to her desertion. Dempsey shared all of her evenings. He was an immense black Labrador retriever picked up as a stray from the roadside shortly after her arrival in Denver. Flopped rug-like on the floor of her bedroom, he had looked at her woefully as she dressed, his intelligent eyes watching every flick of the makeup brush. "I won't be gone long, Demps. That I can promise you," she tried to console him. "Maybe Josie will send you a treat."

Clayton's eyes danced over the abundant richness of Deborah's auburn hair falling loosely to her shoulders. Earlier in the day she had worn it in a chignon at the nape of her neck, very smart and feminine, but he much preferred it this way. She wore a sleeveless, high-necked sequined sheath in autumn gold and carried a complementing shawl. "I must say," Clayton said, seeming about to pounce, "that you look—well, ravishing is the only word that comes to mind."

"You are too kind," Deborah said impersonally. "We must hurry out. My car is parked out front, and the doorman isn't too thrilled with me for leaving it there."

"Any man would be thrilled with you for anything."

Really? thought Deborah cynically. *Put that in writing in the form of a signature on a Hayden contract.*

For a Thursday night, Josie's bar was doing good business. A sizeable crowd, including a number of the strapping regulars who worked in a bottling factory one block away, filled the smoky room, keeping the carrot-haired woman behind the bar busy. Clayton's eyes narrowed against the smoke, assessing the value of the hanging Tiffany lamps, solid brass fittings, mahogany bar and booths, and decided that he could be persuaded to allow Josie's Bar to stay. His decision would depend on the young woman beside him. He winced as the proprietress spotted them and let out a gravelly bellow of welcome.

"Deborah, lass, what a wonderful surprise! Come on up here to the bar. Make way there, lads. Move down a couple of stools. That's right. Here's a pair for ye, Deborah, all nice and warm. Fred!" Josie bellowed toward the end of the bar. "Look who's here!"

A man of short stature, whose outdated, wide-lapeled suit hung from his spare, arthritic frame, thrust a head out from the group discussing the fate of Cutter Street. A wide smile broke across his face when he saw Deborah. "Lovey!" he cried, disengaging himself to join her and the sleekly handsome fellow whose air of superiority was out of place in the friendly merriment of Josie's. What was she doing with a fellow like him anyway? He was too old for her. "How goes it with you, my girl?" He hugged her hard, delighting as always in the clean, youthful smell of her. "Who's this feller?"

"Clayton Thomas, Fred Sims. And this is Josie Peabody. They were the first friends I made in Denver."

"Really?" said Clayton interestedly. His curiosity was piqued. How did a refined woman like Deborah Standridge come to have such devotion to a pair of seedy characters like these? "And what circumstances led to that? I must say, Deborah, you don't seem the type to frequent bars."

"Ye'd be tellin' the truth there!" averred Josie, rolling her eyes as well as her *r*'s. Her father had been Irish, a fact that explained her brogue and speech patterns. "Tell him how it happened, Fred."

Deborah looked on in amusement as Fred straightened his shoulders to tell the story of how they had met during her first week in Denver. "It happened to be a Saturday, and Deborah here, her car was parked down the street a ways. I happened to have strolled out on the sidewalk from my place of business next door, and I see these two roughies on motorcycles pull in on one side of her. The Lord only knows where they come from. We don't see their likes around here too often. Anyways, I watch as Deborah comes out to get into her car to see if these two fellers who are lollin' about on the hood are gonna move. Naturally, when they get a look at her, they don't. They took the keys right outta her hand as she went to unlock the door, and I knew that was the time to call on a few of the boys in Josie's. Sam and Tim, them two fellers with the big shoulders at the end of the bar, they was two that was in here that day, and I rounded them up and a few others, and we went down to rescue Miss Deborah here. They had her pretty shaken up by the time we got down there, no cop in sight, of course. But I'm here to tell you them fellers didn't want no part of what I brung out to Deborah's aid. They took off mighty fast."

"And what was the fate of the keys?" asked Clayton.

"We made 'em a deal," said Fred. "A couple of motorcycles for a set of keys."

"Oh, my. So the three of you have been fast friends ever since."

Catching the patronizing note in Clayton's voice, Deborah said unsmilingly, "Since then I have been grateful for the incident. Otherwise, I might not have known Fred and Josie. Neither would the friends I've brought here."

"Which says something nice about you, Mr. Thomas. Are you new to Denver?" Josie asked.

"No, I've been here before, a number of times. I'm here on business at present."

"What kind of business are you in?" asked Fred politely.

"Banking."

36

"Oh?" said Fred encouragingly, waiting for Clayton to continue.

On the stool beside him, Deborah stirred uncomfortably, and Clayton smoothly changed the subject by remarking on the mirrors that covered the wall behind the rows of liquor bottles. "They must be expensive to repair when things get out of hand on Saturday nights," he suggested, folding his hand around Deborah's. He gave it a conspiratorial squeeze to let her know he wouldn't let the cat out of the bag.

"Never had one broke yet!" Josie said proudly. "We don't allow no hooligans in here. There's enough regulars around most nights big enough to persuade a rowdy customer to take his business elsewhere."

"About the size of that big feller comin' in the door." Fred nodded toward the reflection in the mirror. "Except that he's never been in here before, has he, Josie?"

"Not to my recollection," she said, gazing over Fred's shoulder. "What'll you have, Mr. Thomas? You look like a scotch and water man to me."

"You've hit the nail on the head, Josie. Deborah?"

"Deborah likes a creme de menthe this time of night," Josie answered for her.

On the stool, Deborah had stiffened. In the mirror she caught sight of Dan Parker's silver-streaked head as he made his way toward them, casually dressed in gray sweater and slacks. Clayton had seen him, too, and readied his smile, gripping Deborah's hand tighter when she tried to draw it away. "Hello, Dan," he said affably, swiveling around to greet the tall builder. "Fancy meeting you here."

Chapter Three

I see we had the same idea, at least in part," Dan said, dropping his eyes to Deborah's covered hand. "You made a good point when you asked us that question this morning, Miss Standridge."

"If—" qualified Clayton with a smile at Deborah, "the outcome isn't like knowing the cow of the steak you had for dinner."

Deborah felt her color rising. Daniel Parker had no doubt, either, as to why Clayton had asked her out. And Clayton was making it clear what was at stake if she lost his vote. "It was good of you to come," she said formally, cognizant that Fred had grown very quiet. "Can Josie get you something?"

"A beer, please. Coors." He spoke over her head. "You must be Josie Peabody."

"That I am, sir. And you?"

"Dan Parker." He reached a long arm between Deborah and Fred to shake hands with the plump, good-natured woman whose cheeks were like red plums. "And you're Fred Sims." Dan turned to the much shorter man.

After some deliberation of the proffered hand, during which time Deborah held her breath, Fred took it. "You've got us at a disadvantage, sir, Josie and me. You wouldn't be one of them fellers that's bought this city block, would you?"

Later, Deborah was to compare the sudden hush that fell in the bar, the almost total cessation of speech, to the television commercial about E. F. Hutton. Suddenly every eye and ear seemed to be tuned to their conversation. The men with whom Fred had been talking earlier, the brawny factory workers, disbanded to amble curiously over to them.

"Danny, my boy," said Clayton, releasing Deborah's hand to take a hasty swallow of his drink, "you've just bought us a pack of trouble."

"Fred," Deborah said worriedly, watching the men take position behind Dan, "these gentlemen are here as my guests tonight."

"Well, that's fine, lovey, but I'd still like Mr. Dan Parker here to answer my question, if he'd be so kind."

"I would be so kind, Mr. Sims. Yes, I am one of the investors who has bought this block of Cutter Street," he said pleasantly, ignoring the menacing stir behind him. "Miss Standridge has been trying to convince us that this bar and your establishment are an essential, integral part of the neighborhood, and I wanted to come down and see for myself."

"Well, now, seems to me that'd be mighty hard to do over one bottle of beer. Was that to say that you fellers haven't yet made up yer minds what yer going to do with us?"

"You want us to help make up their minds, Fred?" asked a threatening voice behind Dan.

Deborah slid off the stool, her heart hammering. "Fred—"

"How about an answer to my question?" Fred insisted, his stern inquiry turned to include Clayton Thomas. The financier had reached again for Deborah's hand with the intention of slipping quietly away to leave Dan to deal with the confrontation.

"The final decision has not been made yet," Dan answered. "Suppose you send your friends back to the end of the bar, and you and I can take a stroll next door. I'd like to see Fred's Paper Shack." He nodded toward Clayton. "Mr. Thomas would like to see it, too, no doubt."

"Oh, but I—I can't leave Deborah!" Clayton protested.

"Of course ye can!" Josie scoffed. "This is Deborah's second home. Ye run along. The rest of ye—" she addressed the hefty regulars with a scowl, "go back to your drinking. Your beers are gettin' warm."

To encourage Clayton to accompany Fred and Dan, Deborah gave him a small smile and squeezed his arm, a gesture she hoped had escaped the builder's attention. "Please go with them. I'd like you to see Fred's place. I want to visit with Josie anyway."

When the men had left, Deborah apologized to her friend. "I'm sorry about the near fracas. Clayton Thomas asked me to bring him here tonight, and I thought that maybe, once he had met you and Fred and realized the great condition of the bar, he might be persuaded to at least retain this building when the block is leveled."

"Humph!" grunted Josie. "The only reason a man like that wanted to come here was because he knew that was the only way he'd get the time of day from ye, lass. The other one now, he's a sincere lad. He could have lied about who he was. I'd have much rather have seen ye come in with him. But to tell ye the truth, lass…without Fred next door, I don't know that I'd want the place a'tall. But I thank ye for tryin' to save them for us. Ye've worked hard at it, that I know. And as for that smoother-than-cream fellow, if he's a'thinkin' he can weave himself into your affections by holdin' us over your pretty head, it does me heart good to know he'll be disappointed."

Sipping the creme de menthe, Deborah met the level eye of her friend over the rim of the glass. "He'll be disappointed, Josie."

When the three men appeared later, Fred and Dan were in earnest conversation, Fred energetically reinforcing his sentiments with hand gestures. Clayton looked patently bored. "We must be getting back to the hotel, Deborah," he said briskly, slipping a proprietary arm about her waist and glancing at his gold watch. In the mirror she saw the barely perceptible rise of Dan's black brows. Embarrassed, Deborah rotated around on the bar stool, shaking off Clayton's arm.

"What about your friends down there, Fred?" she asked. "Have they settled down?"

"They ain't a'gonna bother Mr. Parker none, lovey."

"Oh, for God's sake!" snapped Clayton irritably. "Dan can look after himself."

"I appreciate your concern, Miss Standridge," Dan said, his voice disappointingly neutral, conveying nothing. Its indifference provoked a sharp, unexpected pain in her chest. Something of her feeling must have shown, for as Deborah slipped off the bar stool, Dan offered with warmer resonance, "I want to stay and visit awhile longer with Fred and Josie and have another beer."

"As you wish." She blew a kiss to Josie and hugged Fred. "Good night, Mr. Parker," she said, turning to Dan. They stood, almost touching, their glances engaged. "Thank you for taking the time to meet my friends."

"It was a pleasure," he said, and she realized he meant it.

"Well, it was a good thing," said Clayton affably as they drove up under the portiere of the Brown Palace Hotel, "that I arranged for us to have a nightcap in my suite since we were cheated out of one at Josie's. I'll inform the valet to park your car. You go on in and wait for me in the lobby."

"I am afraid I'll have to decline that nightcap, Mr. Thomas. I must get back to Dempsey. He's waiting for me."

41

Clayton's facial features, in spite of their training, went slack. "Dempsey? But I thought you got rid of him."

"Dempsey?" Deborah chuckled as if the idea were laughably absurd. "I could never get rid of Dempsey. Why, I love him!"

"I see," Clayton said frostily, his manner toward her undergoing a distinct change. "That is most unfortunate, not only for you, but for the Hayden firm and your shabby friends. I am sure you realize that."

"Of course, Mr. Thomas, but the price for your vote is too high. Good night."

That night Deborah lay awake for a long time in the starlit brightness of her bedroom. On the floor beside the bed, curled up in his padded basket, Dempsey snored gently. The arresting face of Daniel Parker drifted between her and the stars overhead, shining familiarly through the glass portion of the ingeniously designed roof. She had built the house with money from her inheritance after she had been named head of the urban planning department five years ago.

He didn't care for me at all, she thought, *not from the moment I walked into the meeting. Now he certainly doesn't. He thinks I'm spending the night with Clayton Thomas to get the contract.* She should have been angry, but the idea hurt her. It would be embarrassing when their paths crossed again, a likely possibility once he moved to Denver.

Toward morning, she flounced over on her side, yanked the covers up, and forced him from her mind. *Dan Parker, you can go to blazes!*

At the firm the next morning, Deborah slipped into the back door unnoticed. Today, before the weekend, Randall would probably announce that the decision had been made by Mr. Parker and his associates to select another firm for the project. Never by word or deed would he ever make her feel the slightest bit responsible for the loss of the contract. But the others would. Even Tony Pierson, whose down payment on a new house and the arrival of a second child had drained him financially, could not help but resent the flubbing of a commission that would have guaranteed each of them a handsome Christmas bonus. And John Turner would be intolerable.

Deborah tried to concentrate on a new project, but her thoughts kept returning to the contract's loss. The disappointment of her colleagues was one thing, the loss of the money and challenge to the firm another, but for Fred and Josie, the rejection of the bid was nothing short of a tragedy. Neither of them had anywhere to go or anything to do with the rest of their lives.

Midmorning, Bea's characteristic knock sounded on the door. "You look like somebody waiting to be sentenced to death," the secretary remarked when she entered. "Randall would like to see you. He's in his office with Mr. Parker."

"Mr. Parker? Why did he feel it necessary to come in person to reject the bid?"

"Who says he did?"

"Well, why else would he be here?"

Bea's eyes rounded innocently. "Maybe to tell us that we'd won it."

"What?" Deborah leaped up. "Bea, if you're getting my hopes up on the strength of your never-ending optimism—"

"Which is a trait you would do well to have more of, young lady," Bea reproved loftily. "Now, I'm not about to say another word. Come on. They're waiting."

Deborah knew from the moment she was ushered into Randall's office, where Dan Parker sat with the contents of the mortgage package on the desk before him, that the firm had been awarded the contract. Both men rose as she entered, and the expressions on their faces gave away the good news. Deborah thought her legs would give way from sheer relief. "Congratulations, my dear," said Randall, escorting her to a chair. "Dan has just informed me that the firm has won the bid."

"I think I am going to do a very stupid thing and cry," Deborah said as she sank into the chair.

"Even before we tell you that the corporation not only accepted the conditions of the bid but agreed to charge Fred and Josie only the comparable rent they're paying now for the rest of their working lives?" Dan said, looking down at her with the beginning of a smile.

Schooled most of her life to restrain the expression of natural impulses, Deborah had to grip the arms of the chair to prevent herself from leaping out of it and flinging her arms around Daniel Parker. "You mean it! *Both* get to remain!"

"If they can stand the noise of the wrecking crews."

"Oh, Mr. Parker!"

Dan Parker was not a man easily surprised. He was waiting for her when she seized him, bending his tall, silver-streaked head to better oblige the arms thrown around his neck. He held her with easy competence while they laughed elatedly into each other's eyes, both adrift on a mutual wave of joy at the glad news.

"Thank you," Deborah whispered. "Thank you with all of my heart."

"You're welcome."

"I thought there was no hope, especially after last night. Mr. Thomas wasn't too pleased with me because I—and then I thought that you thought that I—" Deborah drew a relieved breath, catching a woodsy whiff of a fine cologne. "Am I confusing you?"

"Not at all. I have all day."

She liked him, she realized suddenly, gazing up into his eyes.

She liked him a great deal. That was why she had been so hurt. He was so attractive, so tanned and towering and rugged. She felt embraced by a mountain—as if she could stay in the shade and shelter of him all day.

At the desk, Randall cleared his throat loudly. "My dear Deborah, it would seem to me that Mr. Parker has been thanked enough."

"Oh—" Deborah immediately came to herself and withdrew her arms. Dan, with evident reluctance, did likewise. But they were still grinning at each other, still sharing a look of pleasure when Deborah sat down again. She was positively giddy. Turning her laughter to Randall, she checked it sharply. He was lighting his pipe, his attention on the procedure, but beneath the thinly hooded eyes she thought she detected sparks of displeasure. Puzzled, Deborah sobered immediately, her jubilance partially extinguished.

"There is always, of course, a bit of bad news with any good," Randall said to her. "The firm has been awarded the contract on the strength of my assurance that we can have the construction documents ready for Dan to take to the city planning and zoning commission by November twenty-second. That gives us only a little over nine weeks, Deborah. Do you foresee any problem in meeting the deadline?"

"Nine weeks," Deborah repeated, a little dazed. "Well, there certainly won't be time to waste, certainly none for mistakes, but, to answer your question, no, I don't foresee any problem."

"Good," Randall said with satisfaction. "We will, of course, have a party this afternoon in the production room after work. Champagne and caviar seem to be appropriate. I'll have Mrs. Talbert get on the details right away. I regret that you and the other gentlemen will not be able to attend, Dan. I assume you're all flying out today?"

"The others are, but I've rented a town house near Cutter Street until I can make some arrangements for a temporary office. I won't be returning to Phoenix until the site is cleared. Razing will begin Monday. So," he said with a grin at Deborah, "I'd very much like to attend your party, Randall."

"By all means. Deborah, if Mr. Parker has nothing more to discuss with you at present, you may go back to your office. I'm sure you'll want to call Fred and Josie to tell them the good news."

"Why, yes," she said, wondering if she had imagined the cool tone. "They will want to have a party of their own tonight. It should be some wingding." Rising, she could not resist offering a hand to Dan. "Thanks again, Mr. Parker. You won't be sorry for your decision about Fred and Josie, and we'll have those documents ready on the twenty-second."

"I'm counting on that, Miss Standridge. That's why I pushed for the Hayden firm and you in particular as the architect in charge. You're known around town as a lady who meets deadlines. My interim financing arrangements are based on having those documents approved by December fifteenth. Also, it looks as if a steel strike is likely to begin January first. I want my steel ordered and in here by then."

"Whew!" Deborah exclaimed. "No space for a goof of any kind, is there?"

"I'm afraid not. I don't like doing business with this kind of time pressure, but with that steel strike coming and interest rates as volatile as they are, I don't have any choice."

"Which means we don't either," said Randall.

"Well," Deborah said, releasing a deep sigh. "We can only do our best and hope it's good enough." She took back her hand and smiled at Dan. "See you at the party."

On the way back to her office, ridiculously lighthearted that Dan Parker was not returning immediately to Phoenix, Deborah was nonetheless disturbed by her cool dismissal from Randall's office. Perhaps his old-fashioned sense of decorum had been offended when she had thrown herself at Mr. Parker like that. Randall expected a certain standard of behavior from women and had often commented that she was the only "true lady" of her age that he knew. "These modern young women—" he would say, breaking off with distaste. Deborah was at home with all of Randall's opinions. Many of them her parents had shared. The warmth of Dan's handshake was still with her when she picked up the phone to dial Josie's Bar.

Dan backed the luxurious rental car out of the visitor's space in front of the Hayden firm, his thoughts on Deborah Standridge. She was as beautiful as he had expected and as brilliantly talented. Her concept of his headquarters was a masterpiece of design. Not even her devotion to that likeable but seedy pair on Cutter Street had surprised him, certainly not her obvious devotion to Randall Hayden.

He had known beforehand, of course, that the Hayden firm would get the contract. He would have seen to that. As it was, he had been spared having to use his well-known tactics of persuasion. All but one of the five votes cast had been in favor of the Hayden firm.

In the quiet of the sumptuously upholstered car, Dan chuckled aloud. Clayton's had been the only negative vote. Apparently the delectable Miss Standridge had not been among Denver's after-hours delights. He would have loved to have seen the blanching of Clayton's sun-lamp tan when Deborah told him to go fly a kite.

"Deborah, what's keeping you!" exclaimed Bea. "Everybody's waiting for the woman of the hour!"

"Oh, Bea, I am hardly that. Everybody is in on this coup." Deborah gave her hair a final stroke, having decided to brush it out of the businesslike chignon for a more festive look, and began collecting the articles she had used to refresh her makeup.

"You look beautiful!" Bea declared in several octaves above her normal tone. "Was all that done for us?"

"Was all what?" asked Deborah innocently. From the waggish movement of Bea's blue-tinted gray head, it looked as if the secretary had already been at the champagne.

"You know what I'm talking about! Did you get all gussied up just for us or would Daniel Parker be coming to the party?"

"Bea, Mr. Parker was invited. Whether he will come or not, I don't know."

"Oh, my Lord!" screeched Bea. "We have a *romance* going! Didn't I tell you he was something?"

"Yes, you did, and yes, he is," said Deborah, pulling Bea's arm through hers and heading for the door.

When she entered the production room, everyone seemed to be waiting for her except Daniel Parker, she noted as her eyes swept the group. To her intense embarrassment, a cheer went up, made less inhibited by the champagne already flowing. The only somber note in the room was provided by the visage of John Turner, whose smile was definitely strained.

Randall Hayden emerged from the group of celebrants and favored her with a proud smile. "How lovely you look, my dear, but what has happened to your hair?"

It was because of Randall's suggestion when she first came to work for the Hayden firm that Deborah ordinarily wore her hair in a chignon. Now she ran a hand down one luxuriant side of it and said, "Why, I thought I'd wear it long for the party. Has it begun to float around?"

"No, but you know that I prefer a woman's hair to be tidy.

Yours is so…abundant. But never mind that. You must take a bow." He smiled at the group, and Bea handed her a glass of champagne. Randall, raising his, proposed a toast: "To Deborah, who has proved us proud, as they say in the South, and to all of you who worked so diligently to prepare the bid. May our family be even more united and happier than ever."

"Here! Here!" the group chorused, touching glasses.

Deborah, facing Bea, knew from her giggle of delight that Dan had arrived. She had a chance to take her heart in hand and pour a glass of champagne before the deep voice said, "Am I too late to toast the lady?"

"Not at all," she said, turning with the champagne. "I thought you might have changed your mind." He had exchanged the business suit for corduroy slacks and a jacket, a casual statement that somehow said he was looking forward to the evening.

"I wouldn't have done that for any reason," Dan stated, looking directly into her eyes. He touched her glass. "To you," he said softly, drinking, still holding her eyes. Deborah was entranced.

"Glad to see that you could make it, Dan," said Randall, breaking the compelling moment. "What do you plan to do with your weekend?"

"Oh, I'll think of something," Dan replied, smiling and glancing at Deborah.

"I am sure you will. Bachelors of your resources do not seem to have trouble with that sort of thing." He turned to Deborah—pointedly, she thought. "I am looking forward to Sunday, my dear. Two o'clock at my house. I'm having a rather special supper, I think."

"They always are, Randall," Deborah said, suddenly feeling the need to be especially kind to him. The chill was back in his manner. Was it possible he did not like Dan Parker?

Randall directed an explanation to Dan. "We have a bridge foursome that meets every third Sunday. Deborah is quite a player. Do you play, Dan?"

"Not bridge, I'm afraid," the builder answered. There was a moment's silence between the two men before Randall wished them a good evening and moved on to another group.

Dan, observing him walk away, commented, "He is very devoted to you."

Caught in the aftermath of a masculine exchange she had not understood, Deborah said, "Yes, Randall has been like a father to me. He has provided many opportunities for me to prove myself, as with the Parker project." She smiled. "I've been very lucky."

"Oh, I wouldn't say that," said Dan. "I wouldn't say that at all. Will you have dinner with me tomorrow night?"

"Yes," Deborah answered promptly.

The boisterous party at Josie's had been going on for some time, and Deborah was conscious only of the fact that she was a bit intoxicated. "Easy, lass," Josie cautioned as Deborah slid carefully off the bar stool, aided by Dan's steadying hand at her elbow. "She hardly ever drinks," Josie said to Dan. "I'm worried about her getting home. She can't drive in her condition."

"I'll take care of her," Dan said, helping her into her coat. He couldn't help but laugh. She was very funny when she'd had one too many. Unlike some women he knew who became mean and spiteful when drunk, Deborah was appealingly humorous. The expression she gave him now was bewitching in its inebriated innocence, and he drew her protectively into his arms. "I won't let her drive home in this condition. Say good night to the nice folks," he instructed.

"Good night to the nice folks," Deborah obeyed with an infectious laugh. "Does that mean we have to go away now?"

"Yes," Dan said, chuckling. "That means we have to go away now. Good night, Josie, Fred." Dan released an arm to shake hands. "It was a fine evening. I'm glad I was included."

"Since you were the cause of it, you should have been," said Fred. "You'll be taking her home in your car, I suppose? Hers will be fine here."

"Good enough," said Dan. "Come on, lovely lady."

The brisk night air hit her like a splash of cold water. "Mr. Parker," she said with solemn formality, the Southern accent slightly slurred. "I do believe I am inordinately tipsy."

"You can say that again," Dan agreed as he tucked her into the rental car.

"Mr. Parker, I do believe I am inordinately tipsy."

Dan's mouth quirked in amusement as he started the motor. "And I know just the place for you to sleep it off, sweetheart."

"How about right here?" Deborah sighed, laying her head back against the headrest and closing her eyes.

She was awakened when the door was opened on her side of the car. A tall man with silver hair led her along an unfamiliar walk toward a strange door beside a flower bed she had never seen before. "This isn't my house!" she declared in confusion.

"No, it isn't," he said in an unusually deep voice. But then, he was so tall and big. A voice had to come a *long* way to get out of him! "Come into my parlor said the spider to the fly."

That was a nice jingle, thought Deborah as she tottered over the threshold, supported by the tall man's strong arm. "What are you going to do?" she inquired, looking up at a blur of silver.

"Well, now, my lovely, that depends on you," the tall man said, swinging her up in his arms.

Chapter Four

She awoke from the weight of light upon her eyelids. Cautiously, painfully, still struggling up from the nauseating depths of some strange, murky slumber, Deborah lifted first one lid and then the other. There was an unfamiliar ceiling above her head; a white, garish one. Where was her glass roof? Carefully, because some still-functioning center of intellect warned her not to move too fast, Deborah reached over the side of the bed for Dempsey. No Dempsey. Where was he? Where was *she*?

Disregarding caution, she attempted to rise, but the sudden movement detonated an explosion inside her head, forcing her back upon the pillow with a sharp cry of pain. Covering her eyes from the light, she made an effort to think, but that hurt, too. A door opened, bringing the sense of a human presence. A deep, vaguely familiar voice said, "This will make you feel better," and her hands were taken away and the shockingly cold compress positioned over her eyes. "When you feel that you can sit up," the voice went on, "I have some aspirin and tomato juice."

"Dan—?"

"Yes. Don't try to talk. Everything is all right."

After the tomato juice and aspirin, she dozed, and upon awakening again, found the light bearable. Recollection of the night before was making headway through the fog of a headache without shedding much light on how she had come to be in Dan Parker's bedroom. The answer to that could come later. The objective now was to get up.

Deborah rolled off the bed to her feet, coming face-to-face with a disheveled stranger in the mirror. With a shocked gasp, she realized that the starkly pale face and mascara-smudged eyes were hers. She looked down at the crush of wrinkles that was her cream silk shirt and the bottom half of her beige satin slip. She was still in her panty hose. Where were her skirt, her shoes?

"Deborah, what are you doing?"

Very carefully, since too sudden a movement would have risked injury, Deborah rotated in the direction of the question. Dan Parker had come into the room, newspaper in hand, wearing slippers and a blue robe a trifle short for his long runner's legs. Deborah looked away in embarrassment. "I'm looking for my shoes and skirt. I have to go home. Dempsey will be worried about me."

"Dempsey?"

"My dog. He's not used to spending the night outside, and he'll be hungry."

"You're not going anywhere until you have a shower and some breakfast. Then I'll drive you to your car. It's still parked at Josie's. Dempsey will be all right until you get home. Your things are in the closet, and there's a spare toothbrush in the second drawer of the linen cabinet. Do you think you can manage?"

"Yes," Deborah said, afraid to nod her head.

Under the reviving jet of the shower, Deborah recognized that she was beginning to have a new set of feelings about a man. She couldn't remember ever *liking* a man, not since Roger. Except...liking Dan gave her such a pleasant, zestful, good-to-be-alive feeling. She not only respected him, she was physically attracted to him as well, and for her, *that* was a rare response indeed.

Dan was different from the bachelors she was accustomed to seeing—men on their way up who knew the importance of having the right address, the right possessions, being seen with the right woman. In addition to a presentable appearance and professional prestige, she enjoyed what Randall called a "certain air of breeding," appreciated by the socially conscious men in her life.

Their egos might have been considerably dented had they known why she really preferred their type. They, who loved only themselves, were not likely to love her. They were invulnerable to her, her beauty and worth, and she was safe from them and from herself. There was not a Roger among them who might run his Mercedes into a wall because of her.

Not that Dan would, either. But he was the kind of man who would want more from her than just an impressive presence on his arm for an evening out. He had the kind of robust male magnetism that bespoke a healthy enjoyment of sex, and therein lay the problem. Sex was not for her. Of that, she was quite certain.

In the bathroom mirror, Deborah gazed at the much improved reflection of herself. Now that she'd had a chance to make a site analysis of the situation, she could render a plan. And the plan called for backing off from this relationship. Dan's regard was too important to her. They would be working together closely on the project this year; a romance was out of the question under the circumstances.

"Well!" Dan said cheerfully, looking up from the morning newspaper at the small sunlit table in the breakfast nook. He was still in the blue robe, long brown legs crossed. The aroma of fresh coffee and something cheesy baking in the oven filled the kitchen. Sunlight streamed through a sliding glass door that lead to a small patio. "You don't look too bad for a little booze-hound the morning after. How do you feel?"

"Still a little headachy, but much better, thank you. Mr. Parker, I—"

"*Mister* Parker! What's this mister business? You spent the night in my bedroom, Deborah, so that entitles you to call me Dan." He got up, amused, his hands in the pockets of his robe, and moved to where she stood uncertainly in the doorway. "Embarrassed?" He grinned.

"I don't know what happened after the third or fourth Tom Collins. Did I make a complete fool of myself?"

"Not in my opinion or anybody else's, for that matter. You were awfully cute, and funny as the devil. You led a sing-along, sang 'The Ramblin' Wreck from Georgia Tech,' and demonstrated the polka, but other than that—"

Deborah closed her eyes. "Oh me, oh my. Thank God Randall Hayden wasn't there."

"And one other little thing. Everybody knows you left with me, so I can't speak for what that will do for your reputation."

"Why didn't Bea suggest I stay at her place?"

Dan looked a bit sheepish. "I was scared to death somebody would come up with that idea."

It took Deborah's weakened mental state a few seconds to assimilate that information. Then she gingerly risked a laugh. "Er, uh...what happened after you brought me here?"

"Not a damned thing, unfortunately. Now help yourself to coffee. There's also some more juice, if you like, and go out to the patio. You'll find a fine Rocky Mountain morning out there. I'll go get dressed and then we'll have some breakfast."

With a steaming cup of coffee, Deborah went out on the

patio. A fine September morning, crisp and clear, was indeed waiting. Majestic mornings like these always made her glad that she had come to Colorado. Dan's town house faced west, and this morning no smog obscured the snow-capped peaks in the distance. Deborah breathed deeply of the freshness and the aroma of breakfast baking and pulled out a wrought-iron chair. As she sat down, she noticed a pair of running shorts and socks and a sweatshirt draped over the railing. *He's already been out jogging*, she thought, remembering that last night Dan had told her the town house was close to a track.

"Ready for a little breakfast?" her host asked, coming out on the patio with placemats, silverware, and salt and pepper shakers. "We'll eat out here, if that's all right with you." He was in jeans, a blue denim shirt, and tennis shoes. There was a vitality about him that matched the morning, an exuberance of masculine vigor and spirit that filled her heart and made her smile. He truly was a devastating man.

"You seem very practiced at all of this," Deborah accused him archly as he began to set the small wrought-iron table.

"Well, I've had quite a bit of experience at this sort of thing."

"I'll just bet you have," she said wryly.

He answered with his deep, warm laugh, blue eyes twinkling down at her from beneath the expressive black brows, his smile easy and approving. "You know, you're not at all bad looking." Before she could reply, he bent down and deposited a full kiss on her open mouth. "That will do you until tonight," he said easily, straightening up. "Now I'll get that breakfast."

It was a soothing, satisfying combination of eggs and cheese and bread baked into a firm custard topped with bacon. "This is delicious." Deborah sighed. "Where did you learn how to cook?"

"I can't remember when I *didn't* know how to scramble

something up for the table," Dan replied. "My mother died when I was barely out of diapers, and my dad came back from Korea with a leg shot off and a lot of bad memories he never learned to deal with. It was up to me to look after us. As a bachelor, I've been grateful for the fact that I'm pretty proficient in the kitchen."

It was said without the least intent to elicit pity, but Deborah's heart was suddenly wrung by the vision of a solicitous little boy, barely tall enough to stand at the kitchen cabinet, attempting to put together a family meal. She could feel herself being pulled deeper into this involvement, and her resistance was weakening. She must get out now before she took another bite. "Uh, Dan, about tonight. Could we have a rain check? I feel awful, and I have so much to do at home. I have a dozen errands to run and half the day is already gone—" She bit her lip. What a lame package of excuses!

Dan wasn't buying it either. The blue eyes rested steadily on her as he sipped his coffee, waiting for her to come to terms with whatever she was trying to tell him. "I take that back," she said abruptly, looking off toward the mountains. "My real reason in not wanting to see you is that I don't think it's a good idea to mix social and business lives. We'll be working together closely this year, and our professional relationship could suffer if—if we became involved emotionally."

"You must be awfully sure of my intentions to become... involved emotionally."

Deborah caught the mocking note and blushed. She supposed she deserved that, but she intended to stick to her guns. She said directly to Dan, "If I am wrong, then I misread the signals, and I apologize."

Dan set his cup down carefully. "You didn't misread the signals, Deborah, and you may be right about mixing social and business lives. But I want to see you again. Maybe I already am involved. I think you are, too."

"No," she said, shaking her head. "You're wrong. At least I'm not so involved that I can't pull out now." She wiped her mouth and slipped the napkin under the edge of her plate. "You've been so kind," she said formally. "I'll help you to clear away the dishes, and then if I could impose upon you to drive me to my car..."

Dan's reaction was to cut another piece of the breakfast custard. "Sit down, Miss Standridge. I haven't finished my meal and neither have you. If you're like most women living alone, you probably won't eat another bite until I pick you up at seven, so eat up. You'll have to give me instructions on how to get out to your place. I'm looking forward to spending a quiet *business* evening with the architect in charge of my project. There are a few revisions in the plans I would like to suggest. Nothing major," he said when he saw her eyes widening.

"You're splitting hairs!" she charged.

"That could be so," Dan said unconcernedly, taking a big bite of the custard. "But then that's a prerogative of the client."

Nice, very nice, thought Dan that evening as he pulled into the circular drive leading to Deborah's house. *A little remote, though, for a girl living alone.* Before ringing the doorbell, he admired the architectural distinction of the house, the sensitive attention to silhouette, particularly at the juncture of building to sky. The location of the house at the foot of a mountain some distance from neighbors was symbolic of Deborah somehow, or at least his preliminary impression of her. She required both being sheltered and being left alone.

"Good evening," Deborah said in answer to the push of the brass doorbell. Behind her, its mellow peal still resonated throughout the house, like the chimes of a fine old clock. From the far regions came the bark of a dog, Dempsey, no doubt, confined to the kitchen until the greetings were over. "Did you have trouble finding me?"

"Not at all. This is very beautiful," Dan said, his glance indicating the house. "Your design, I imagine?"

"Yes. I was afraid that you might not get to see much of the exterior since the sun sets so quickly now. Please come in. Those are for me?"

He had brought her a dozen red roses. He had never been a man for giving flowers to women, but he very much wanted to bring her something lovely and special tonight. She was the kind of woman to whom a man brought lovely and special things.

"They are so beautiful, Dan," she exclaimed softly, lifting the long-stemmed roses out of the green tissue paper in the long box. Her face glowed with the childlike pleasure that had so moved him last night. "Would you mind mixing a drink for yourself?" she asked. "The bar is there, and I believe you'll find anything you want. I must get a vase for these."

He assured her that he could manage and went to the bar, but his attention was still on Deborah. He admired the long, straight back and elegant legs as she walked into the dining room to select a vase from a lighted cabinet filled with glittering crystal and china. The entire house had a quiet air of tasteful opulence.

"I love roses," she said, coming back carrying the buds and vase. While he poured his drink, she arranged the flowers on the coffee table.

Dan realized that he had spoken only a few words since arriving, that he had been unable to do anything but drink her in. "Roses become you," he said solemnly, observing the lovely blooms near her face. "May I pour you anything?"

"Only a pitcher of water from the bar for these, if you don't mind. There's one above your head there. Last night should do me for quite a while." She laughed. "I'll have a glass of wine with dinner. When I arrange these, I'll go get Dempsey. He has to be kept in the kitchen until guests are settled; then he's allowed to come in and say hello. He has pretty good manners for a fellow with no formal education."

"You mean he didn't go to obedience school?" asked Dan, handing her the pitcher. "What breed is he?" She was wearing a sheer navy dress over its own strapless underslip, which left little doubt of the fullness of her breasts. A prim narrow band of white satin, much like a clergyman's collar, caught the dress at the neck, chastening its allure. Her hair, rich and full, swept away from a well-defined widow's peak in an auburn tempest of waves and curls. At her ears were pearls of impressive size, encircled with diamonds. Dan wondered who had bought her those, or if she purchased her own jewelry. There was so much about her he wanted to know.

"...I picked him up as a stray by the side of the road," Deborah was saying when he took his thoughts back to her explanation about the dog. "He was starving and had been terribly abused. I'd never had a dog, nor a pet of any kind, actually. I had no idea if I could take care of him, but I opened the car door and invited him in. I knew I was taking a chance. My mother would have had a hissy, but I felt so sorry for him. As it's turned out, we've been very good for each other. He's been no trouble at all. Shall I go get him?" Deborah asked.

"By all means," said Dan.

Deborah got to her feet, encased in navy satin shoes, he noticed, and left the room. While she was gone, Dan sipped his martini and reflected on the insight into her disposition he had just been given.

After meeting Dempsey, who seemed to like Dan at first sniff, he was taken on a tour of Deborah's house. Again, Dan thought how well it suited her. It was a combination of contemporary and traditional design, with gracious rooms quietly and elegantly furnished. For a young woman not yet thirty, Dan noted, she had acquired an enviable collection of fine things. He was amused and somehow pleased at her hesitancy, disguised with a flippancy unnatural to her, to show him her bedroom. *She's afraid of me,* he thought, *afraid of what could happen between us. Why?* She did not seem a woman fearful of men, only of him. He must learn why.

"Deborah, it's ingenious!" he said in appreciation when the double doors were opened to her bedroom. It was a room of wide, graceful proportions, decorated in soothing blues and greens, furnished in rich woods. But it was the roof line that intrigued him. Instead of a flat plane, it jutted out at an oblique angle to the night sky, leaving a wide but protected portion of glass directly above the king-sized bed. Moonshine and starlight flowed into the room. Dan could imagine lying on the bed, lost in the illusion of floating among the clouds and stars. "Surely something inspired you to design the roof like that!"

"Well, yes, but it's as silly as singing 'The Ramblin' Wreck from Georgia Tech'!"

"Try me," he urged.

"When I was a little girl, I used to think how exciting it would be to go camping and lie out at night gazing at the stars. There has always been something about space and nature that has appealed to me. I used to think that when I *got grown,*" she underlined the choice of words with a self-conscious laugh, "I would learn how to camp and hike and fish. Not hunt. I could never hunt."

"You didn't go camping when you were a little girl?" His tone was quiet and encouraging.

"Oh, heavens, no! My parents didn't allow it. Besides, they were not young when I was born, and were far past the age to rough it by the time I was able to do so. So when I *got grown,*" she laughed again, "I compromised with my little-girl fantasies and built this room so that I could lie here at night and see the stars."

"Then you never did learn to fish or hike or camp?"

"No." She smiled. "I've never known anyone who could teach me."

"No one?" Dan asked, lifting his brows at the question.

"Well, yes, there was one man, someone I knew long ago," Deborah said, puzzled by the query and thinking of Roger, "but I was...still a little girl then." She changed the subject and led him from the room.

She was taken to a restaurant overlooking a deep gorge. Directly across from the glass alcove where they sat was the summit of another mountain, its cap of last year's snow glistening in the moonlight. Deborah thought how alike they were: the mountain across the way and the man sitting across from her, his hair gleaming like silver beneath the softly defused lights.

"Why did you choose Denver for the location of your headquarters, Dan?" Deborah asked after they had ordered. Both had chosen rainbow trout, caught that day from the cold stream gurgling far below in the rocky, narrow ravine, which in daylight could be seen from their window.

"The labor force is easier to deal with in Denver, and it's central to the locations I hope to be developing during the coming years. What about you? How did a girl from Savannah happen to land here?"

Deborah explained that Randall Hayden had offered her a job right after graduation from college.

"I'm surprised some guy had not already put an engagement ring on your finger," said Dan, taking a sip of his martini and noting the sudden flush of color in Deborah's cheeks.

Her eyes dropped to the wineglass as she reached for it. "At the time, marriage was not for me," she said.

"Has it ever been?"

"No. I'm not the marrying type. My career means too much to me. I could never combine the two. Neither would be successful."

"So you've foregone marriage for your work?"

"Yes." She smiled faintly. "You seem to have done the same."

"Appearances can be deceiving," Dan said, offering no further comment on the subject. He brought up Clayton Thomas. "I've made an offer to buy him out," he said. "I don't approve of his business tactics. I apologize for the fact that you had to be subjected to the particular kind of strong-arm maneuvers he's capable of."

"They didn't work, you know."

"I know," Dan said with a smile.

Her heart felt lighter instantly. She laughed aloud.

"Tell me," he demanded, smiling more broadly, affected by her laughter.

Grinning, Deborah related the details of how she had used Dempsey as an excuse to avoid the rest of the amorous evening Clayton had planned. "You mean he never knew that Dempsey was a dog?" Dan asked in an explosion of laughter. Deborah shook her head, and their joined mirth filled the glass alcove.

For the rest of the evening, their conversation was light and enjoyable. No mention was made of revisions in the plans. Only as Dan was driving her home did there come a feeling of disquiet between them. Dan sensed Deborah's tension and knew she was worrying about how to get rid of him tactfully without causing offense. He did not intend to make it easy for her. He had to find out why she was afraid of him.

In the circular drive, her hand went immediately to the door handle as the car stopped. "No need to walk me to the door," Deborah said lightly, disregarding the manners that dictated the contrary. "Thank you for a lovely evening. I enjoyed every minute of it."

"Deborah—" Dan reached for her hand and held it in a gentle vise. "I most certainly do have to walk you to the door. Furthermore, I want to make sure everything is all right in the house before I leave you."

"You're thinking of burglars?" She laughed thinly. "With Dempsey in the house?"

He did not comment on the fact that burglars intent on breaking into a house knew how to deal with a dog. "Why are you so nervous? You're afraid of me, aren't you? And your fear has nothing to do with what we talked about earlier—mixing personal and business relations."

"Afraid of you?" Deborah chortled. "Of course not. That's ridiculous. I—"

"Then ask me in for a nightcap."

In the darkness of the car, a narrow band of light from the portico fell directly across his eyes. The challenge in them was hard and clear. Dan's fingers moved to her wrist, and Deborah knew he could feel the race of her pulse. Why *was* she so afraid? Nothing had to happen unless she let it. With mock solemnity, Deborah said, "Very well. Won't you come in for a brandy, Mr. Parker?"

Dempsey greeted them at the door, wagging his tail and sniffing the doggy bag with the remains of the boneless trout she had saved for him. "Please help yourself to brandy," Deborah invited, "while I give Dempsey his treat."

"I believe I'll wait for you, Deborah," Dan said quietly. "Hurry back, won't you?"

In the kitchen, watching Dempsey wolf down the trout, Deborah came to an astonishing conclusion. She didn't really *want* to discourage Dan's…physical attentions. The thought was so novel, her mind couldn't pursue it. She took another tack. If Dan tried to make love to her, and it looked as though he would try—if not tonight, soon—what would she do? Regardless of these new and startling feelings, the situation was clearly impossible. How could she cool this relationship gracefully? What could she say? Do? She'd never had this sort of problem before. Dan was no Clayton Thomas…

"Deborah, what's the matter?"

He had come into the kitchen, and she was suddenly aware of the tears in her eyes, easily visible under the harsh glare of the overhead lights. "Oh, rats!" she said.

Dan gently turned her to face him. "Tell me what's disturbing you. Why are you afraid of what's happening to us?"

"It has nothing to do with you."

"What then? Does it have anything to do with the past, something you're afraid I might not understand?"

She stared up at him, the amber eyes bright and searching. "What if it does?"

"The past is yours, Deborah, not mine. It's not for anyone else to forgive or remember. It forged you, made you the woman you are now, and that's all that matters."

"Oh, but Dan—" She moved out from under his hands and walked into the living room to kinder lights and the familiar comfort of possessions brought from the home in Savannah, to the tribute of tall red roses in the crystal vase, a mockery now.

65

"You see," she said, clasping her hands for courage, taking a breath, swallowing at the sadness twisting her vocal cords, "I am one of those women who can't, who can't—"

Dan drew her back against him, resting his chin on the burnished crown of her head. He could feel the taut sorrow in her, the struggle with pain. He was beginning to suspect the nature of her torment and was relieved that it was not as he had thought. "Are you sure you want to go on with this? It's not necessary, you know."

He lowered his head and covered her lips with his own. Unhurriedly, patiently, Dan began to sensually vanquish her fears. He must not give in to his own hunger, he thought. Not yet. He must play her easily, gently—get her ready for him, for herself. Tenderly, Dan traced her lips as if they were the petals of a rose, the delicate wings of a butterfly. Even more tenderly, he tasted them. "Deborah," he whispered, his breath warm on her mouth, "don't worry about loving me. I want to love you. Let me show you how wonderful, how lovely you are."

"No—" she whispered, although even she doubted that she meant it.

"Yes, Deborah. Let me show you the kind of woman you are." Lifting her up in his arms, he carried her up the stairs effortlessly. At the double doors, he paused. "You don't really want me to leave, do you?"

"No," she answered, and there was no doubt in her voice now.

Chapter Five

Deborah did not want to go to Randall's bridge party. She dressed with indifference, choosing from habit clothes that would please him. Randall had decided opinions about what women should wear. In his view bridge called for cashmere sweaters, worn with a single strand of pearls, and wool skirts. Pumps, of course, and perhaps a scarf to tie back the hair. She ought to mind more than she did, Deborah thought. But the truth was, Randall's dictatorial meddlesomeness was so like that of her parents that it served to remind her of their way of showing their love and concern.

Knotting the paisley scarf that complemented the sweater and skirt she had chosen, Deborah grinned at herself in the mirror. Her eyes shone, her skin seemed to glow. The look of love. But how could she be in love with a man she'd only known for four days? Still, everyone there tonight—and especially Randall, who knew her so well—was bound to know something extraordinary had happened.

Well, miracles had that effect. She twirled before the mirror with a laugh, unabashedly admiring her figure, happy that it turned heads. If she wasn't in love, this was certainly the next best thing.

Arising from his rug-like sprawl on the floor, Dempsey

watched his mistress with a quizzical tilt to his head. "Oh, Demps!" Deborah hugged him impulsively, heedless of dog hair on her clothes. "You like him, don't you? Isn't he simply wonderful?"

She had awakened that morning to the sound of water splashing in the shower. She had stretched euphorically, sensuously, then burrowed once again under the covers to relive the ecstacy of the night before. Dempsey was on his pallet. Dan must have already been downstairs to put him outside from the kitchen where he had been confined for the night, then allowed him back in. Deborah smiled to herself under the covers. He was a man who could take care of things, could make himself at home. He had found the soap, towels, the supply of new toothbrushes she kept on hand for guests. When he finished dressing, he would probably go downstairs, bring in the Sunday paper, make coffee, and feed Dempsey. *What a man!* She sighed and dozed off again.

When next she opened her eyes, the sunlight was streaming through her special window. She showered and dressed hurriedly, *her* morning for jeans this time. She didn't want to miss another minute of being with him, and he must be fed a hearty, man-pleasing breakfast.

"Good morning, Dan."

She'd found him sitting at the breakfast bar with the Sunday papers, and her heart had thudded when the silver head turned. Dempsey was at his feet, obviously fed, or he would have been banging his empty bowl. The kitchen was fragrant with the smell of coffee. "You'll stay for breakfast, won't you?"

He had gotten up from the stool and gone to her, and with profound tenderness had taken her face between his big hands. She felt the painful, pleasurable throb, the vital hunger that he had incited the night before, and returned the deep, full, satisfying kiss. "Yes," he said.

She prepared the Southern breakfast that had pleased her father every Sunday morning of his life: ham and eggs, grits, and red-eye gravy for the homemade biscuits. As she stirred and hummed while Dan read the paper, she only hoped he *liked* Southern breakfasts. Her worry vanished when she set his plate before him.

"Grits!" He sighed with pleasure. "And red-eye gravy!"

"How do you happen to know about grits and red-eye gravy?"

His eyes were on the napkin he shook out for his lap. "I've done a lot of building in the South," he said.

Dan had not wanted her to go to Randall's bridge party. He suggested they spend the day together, go for a walk in the woods, buy some steaks, and cook them on the outdoor grill for dinner.

"I can't do that, Dan," she had said with gentle resolution. "These Sunday bridge suppers mean so much to Randall. They're the highlight of his week, and it would be difficult for him to find a fourth this late in the day." As much as she had wanted to cancel, Deborah had been unwilling to disappoint the man she loved like a father. She tried to define their relationship to Dan. "He's been my guide and mentor, my confidant and guardian ever since the first day I set foot in the Hayden firm. He took such a chance with me, Dan, when he named me head of the urban planning department immediately following my internship. He's always supported me, as he proved the other day with the Fred and Josie issue. I have so few opportunities to repay him, to express my appreciation for all he's done for me. That's why I can't cancel this evening."

"You repay him, Deborah, by being the best urban designer

in the state. You've brought a lot of business to the Hayden firm. As for his support of you about Fred and Josie, he pretty well knew he was safe with that gesture. He knew how badly we wanted your designs."

"You don't like Randall, do you?" she had asked slowly, disappointment twisting in her chest.

"He seems so possessive of you. I suppose I can understand that since he's been a widower for so long and has no children. He dotes on you as the daughter he never had. But there can be danger in too much possession."

Deborah had dropped the subject, but they managed the walk in the woods, taking Dempsey. Dan kept a pair of boots in the trunk of his car for site inspections, and he held her hand as they tramped along the edge of the foothills behind her house.

"Tomorrow night then?" he asked as he was leaving. She had looked up at him, so crisp against the background of the blue and gold day, and nodded. "I'll call you at the office about a time and place." Tilting her chin, he had kissed her, not once but several times as autumn leaves swirled around them.

Now she made a sorrowful face in the mirror. "Oh, Dan, I want to be with you tonight!"

The telephone rang on the nightstand. "I miss you already," Dan said. "Did I thank you for a fine day?"

Deborah smiled in tender reflection. "Did I thank you for last night?"

"In the best possible way. Good night, Deborah."

She was a few minutes late, a tardiness that provoked a faint line of disapproval between Randall's fair brows when he opened the door of his Victorian-style residence to her. "It's all right, my dear," he said reassuringly, as if her "hello" had been a lengthy apology. "Traffic wreaks havoc with the most punctual among us, even on a quiet Sunday." He kissed her cheek, re-marking, "What a delightful perfume. I like it almost as much as I do my favorite, which you usually wear. You look lovely. Come on in and greet everyone. Naturally, everybody is here. What shall I get you for an aperitif?"

Good heavens, what have I done? she wondered in surprise as she followed Randall into the library where a fire had been lit and the bridge table set up. The others, a man and a woman in middle age, both lawyers, were at the fire with their drinks. They, too, had just arrived and were relieving the chill of the sudden cold front that had blown down from the Rockies. Deborah gave the evening her best, but she found the conversation dull and the play boring. She was concerned about Randall's cool reserve toward her, carefully concealed from the others by his impeccable manners.

"Deborah, would you mind waiting for a few moments," he requested when the evening finally drew to an end. "I have something to discuss with you that can't wait until morning."

Once the guests were seen off, Randall suggested, "Let us go back to the fire, my dear. I'll not keep you long. You look tired."

Deborah glanced at him sharply. Did she? Or was that an implication of some kind? His manner was so strange. Depressed, Deborah linked an arm through his. "What is it, Randall? Have I offended you in some way? You must tell me."

He seemed mollified by her taking his arm and said in a conciliatory tone, "Forgive an old man who loves you as if you were his very own. I could not bear it if anything happened to you. You are the solace of my old age. Without you, I could not go on."

"Randall, dear—" In dismay, Deborah stared at the

pain-shadowed eyes, the hurt mouth. "Whatever has given you the idea that something will happen to me?"

"Before we discuss that," he patted her hand, "let's have some brandy to take the chill off our bones and—perhaps my words."

Deborah rarely drank after dinner, but she accepted the snifter of brandy and watched as Randall lowered his slight, brittle frame into a velvet high-backed chair the twin of hers. With a frowning interest in the swirl of brandy, he cleared his throat and began, "Bea tells me that you left Josie's Friday night with Dan Parker, and that you were…quite inebriated. I must confess to you frankly, my dear child, that I have been very concerned about where he took you. I can't imagine that he knew where you lived on such short acquaintance, and you were obviously not in a state to direct him."

Deborah set down the snifter of brandy untasted. "Randall, I'm sorry, but that really is none of your business."

"I was afraid you might respond that way, so, lest you think that I am prying into your dealings with men like some—*voyeur*, let me assure you that I have a reason for asking."

"I am anxious to hear it."

"I sense, deep in my heart, where I've always unerringly been warned about matters dearest to me, that Dan Parker will hurt you, Deborah."

"Dan—? Hurt me? Why would he do that?" she asked, seeing Randall flinch at the familiar use of the name.

"Dan Parker is a man to whom business means everything. His sole interest in life is in making money. There is no room for anything or anyone else in it, certainly not the presence of a wife and children. Dan Parker is still unmarried at thirty-eight. That ought to suggest something to you."

"It suggests that perhaps he has never found the woman he wishes to marry," she said quietly.

"Do you believe for a moment that you might be that woman? Oh, my dear child, believe me, you are not. Why, Dan Parker is only interested in... the lowest sort of woman. I'm surprised your research did not reveal that when you were designing his headquarters. Certainly you must have learned that he has kept steady company with the actress Alicia Dameron for years."

"I never pay much attention to the public reputations of well-known people. It's easy to be misled." She had herself in mind when she spoke. It was possible that Dan, too, had used social subterfuge. But she had not known he was a womanizer. She had not known about Alicia Dameron. Where, she wondered, had Randall gotten his information?

"And you are hoping to become the one woman to supplant the others?" Randall's exasperation produced a blunt tone. "Deborah, you must not delude yourself. You are to Dan Parker what some new and different *objet d' art* is to a collector—a collector, I might add, whose origins were in poverty. The blush of owning a Rembrandt wears off quickly to a man whose sole delight in possessing it is the ability to purchase it."

"Randall, that is quite enough!" said Deborah, getting up, aware that she was shaking from both anger and fright.

"My dear child, I am sorry," Randall said hastily, his voice softening. "I beg you to bear with me. All I am saying is that you are an original. He has never met a woman like you before. Do have a seat, please, and hear me out?"

Deborah resumed her seat. "If you are worried that Dan will love me and leave me—isn't that a risk one takes in any relationship?"

"Ahhh." Randall drew it out slowly, leaning toward her. "That question brings me to my point. Do you think you have the stamina to take another deep hurt? You know how broken you were when you first came to the firm. It's taken years to put you back together, and we've managed to do that by directing your energies toward the fulfillment of a creative destiny. If you were to—heaven forbid—fall in love with Dan Parker and he were to abuse that regard, what would that do to you, Deborah?"

Deborah knew that he could discern from the sudden rigidity of her features, the silence that met his question, that his shot had hit home. "You are involved with him already, aren't you?" Randall ventured softly.

"Yes," she said.

"I knew it! I knew it!" He leaped up with surprising agility and in distress paced away from the fire. "I knew that he had gotten to you already, the scoundrel!"

"He hasn't *gotten* to me, and he isn't a scoundrel! You've no basis on which to distrust him so deeply, Randall," Deborah asserted, but she felt unsettled by a nameless disquiet and looked away from Randall to the fire. Without his composure, he seemed as exposed and vulnerable as a featherless bird. "I'm sorry if my seeing Dan disturbs you, but I am a grown woman. I can take care of myself."

Suddenly still, Randall subjected her to a long deliberation. "Will it make any difference in the care you take of yourself, my dear, if I tell you that I have recently made a new will. You are my heir. Upon my death, the firm and all its assets go to you."

Deborah sat speechless, unmoving. Only the merry gossip of flames broke the tense, startled silence. "Randall, that is far too generous."

"That's for me to decide. You are to be my successor. I've made my decision. Now, my dear, I must see you to the door. I am very weary tonight. No, not another word," he admonished when she was about to speak. "Silence is best for reflection. We'll have occasion to discuss this again."

Under the stars, Deborah lay awake thinking about the amazing revelations of the last twenty-four hours. It was true that Randall had an uncanny perception of people, their motives and fears. But he was wrong about Dan. Dan would never hurt her, not deliberately. He possessed too much of the compassion that often comes with great strength, too much of the gentleness so frequently found in big men.

He had given her an incomparable gift—a new knowledge of herself. He had made possible a choice she had subconsciously foresworn. Intimacy, marriage, children. All that had seemed too risky, too dangerous. They offered too many ways to fail, to hurt others and to be hurt herself. She couldn't afford that. Her career had provided a satisfying alternative, and only rarely had she thought of a future and old age without the love of a husband and family. Now Dan had freed her to consider other possibilities.

How ironic that the two men she most admired should have warned her about each other on the same day! How sad that they didn't like each other. Why, Randall had even used that astounding disclosure about the will as an inducement to keep her from seeing Dan. Well, she had news for him! Inheriting the firm would never be enticement enough to give up Dan…*if* she should ever love him.

At the town house, Dan stretched out his long legs before the fire. Occasionally, his knees bothered him now, the result of several injuries he had suffered while playing lineman on his high school football team. He was treating himself to a cigar, a rare luxury, but tonight he was in need of extra comfort. His earlier five-mile jog around the nearby track had not produced an answer to a troublesome question. Staring into the fire, he smoked and thought. By the time the cigar and fire had burned low, Dan had decided how to deal with Deborah Standridge. The best plan would be first to get her to fall in love with him. And then he would spring the surprise.

Monday, which Deborah had anticipated happily, was not off to a good start. At the meeting she called to assign the construction documents for the Parker project, John Turner created a scene. These were the mechanical, electrical, structural, and architectural drawings that Dan Parker would be taking to the city planning and zoning office November twenty-second to ensure that the plans complied with Denver's building and public safety codes.

"Now let me see if I understand you correctly." John spoke each word distinctly. "You are proposing that I wait until you are finished with the architectural drawings of the eight support columns before I am to begin the structural specifications for them?"

"That is correct," Deborah said patiently. "If you look at my original rendering of the lobby, you'll see that there are certain aesthetic considerations about the columns requiring a detailed set of architectural drawings from which to figure the structural computations. That's why I don't want you to work from the original rendering."

"Would that be because you don't trust me to compute them accurately without your blasted drawings, *Miss* Standridge?"

"John," Deborah sighed, "please do not reduce this meeting to a battleground. Where do you get such ideas? We all know that you're the best structural engineer in town." Immediately, she regretted the poor choice of compliments. John's lip curled sardonically.

"Thank you, Deborah," he said with an acerbic smile. "How neatly you manage to keep me in my place. May I humbly remind you that by asking me to wait for your drawings, you could put me behind in my own schedule?"

"No, I won't. You can work on the other structural specifications. I'll begin the drawings for the columns right away and have them to you by next Monday. I wouldn't insist that you use them if those columns weren't such a vital part of the headquarters building. But exposed as they are in the atrium, surely you can understand why it's important that every feature be just right. They're the focal point of the whole design!"

"They're nothing but decorative folderol." John snorted. "They impede the flow of traffic."

"They *aid* the flow of traffic, John!" intervened Tony Pierson. "Just look at the rendering!"

"No thanks. I've been told to wait for the drawings." He stood up, tall and thin. "How long did you say we have on this package?"

Sickened and appalled by the man's unadulterated dislike of her, Deborah answered, "Nine weeks from today. That's when Mr. Parker needs them. Once they've been approved, the steel can be ordered and work on the site begun—"

"Don't tutor me on the ins and outs, the procedures of the building industry, Deborah. I've been dealing with it considerably longer than you have." He favored the group with a bitter smile. "Well, good mawnin' yawl. Doncha tawk about me when ahm gawn, ya heah!" he said, imitating Deborah's accent, and strolled from the conference room.

There was an embarrassed silence when he had gone. "He gets more jealous of you every year, Deborah," Tony maintained.

Deborah mulled over Tony's remark on the way to her office.

Each year John Turner did seem to become more intolerant of her success. His professional jealousy was alienating him from everyone in the firm, perhaps might even endanger his job if Randall were to learn of it. Randall prided himself on running a company that was like a happy family. Discordant notes were not allowed.

Deborah did not want John's position in the firm jeopardized because of her. She felt a strange sympathy for him and even appreciated some of the engineer's qualities that were often overshadowed by his blatant antipathy toward her. There was no one in the firm more loyal to Randall, no one more hard working or dependable than John. Because he had worked for Randall so long and because he held two degrees—engineering and architecture, a notable accomplishment in itself—John had been bitterly disappointed five years before when the urban design department had gone to Deborah. Long divorced, growing older, lonelier, and more frustrated, he seemed to nurse his grudge against her as if it were the only source of comfort in a cold and alien world.

The phone was ringing as she entered the office. "Deborah," Bea said on the line, "would you mind talking to this woman from Phoenix? She is trying to reach Dan Parker with an urgent message and insists on speaking to someone who works directly with him."

"A woman? All right. Put her on. Is she his secretary?"

Deborah recognized one of Bea's dramatic pauses. "Hardly, dear," she said after an appropriate amount of silence. "It's Alicia Dameron, the actress."

Good ol' Bea; she could never resist an occasion for dramatics, thought Deborah in annoyance. She had the sensation of her blood having just frozen. "Then, by all means, put her on," Deborah said evenly.

Alicia Dameron's famous voice did not project the slightest inflection of urgency. It was vivacious, chatty, and confiding, the kind of voice used for old friends. "I hope you'll excuse me for using you as a go-between for Dan and me," Alicia said, "but there's no answer at his town house, and I didn't know where else to reach him. He told me your firm was handling the project he's working on there. May I leave a message for him with you?"

Deborah, remembering the actress from a scene in one of her movies some years ago, could picture the petite, Barbie-doll actress talking on a phone by her swimming pool. She could see the silver blond hair carelessly secured behind shell-pink ears, the devastating beauty of the blue eyes, the perfect, tanned little figure barely covered by a very small bikini. A paralyzing jealousy swept over her.

"Are you there?" Alicia's tone held a merry note of concern.

"I'm here," Deborah answered stiffly. "I'll be talking with Mr. Parker sometime this afternoon and will pass on your message. Does he have your number?"

"Indeed he does!" Alicia laughed gaily. "Tell you what— just have that dear man call me. I want to tell him the good news myself. And my dear, tell him that if he doesn't call me by tonight, he's in big trouble. Emphasize that: *big* trouble!" Her laughter tinkled like a crystal bell.

Deborah tried to settle down to work at the drawing board in her office but could not concentrate. Alicia Dameron's merry voice, its intimate reference to Dan, played over and over in her mind. She was interrupted constantly by the ring of the telephone and by members of the project team with questions about their work. Finally, with an exasperated sigh, Deborah pushed the intercom button. "I'm going home, Bea. I can't get any work done around here. Mr. Parker will be calling sometime today. Please see that he gets this message from Alicia Dameron."

She relayed Alicia's words and heard Bea's sharp intake of breath. "Dan Parker doesn't seem the kind of man to take that kind of domineering from any woman."

"Alicia Dameron isn't any woman, Bea. Be sure and tell Randall that I've left. And when Mr. Parker calls, tell him to telephone me at home."

Deborah irritably pulled her hair out from under the collar of the ultrasuede jacket that was part of the blue ensemble she had selected for her date with Dan. Randall was quite right when he said she should wear her hair in a neckline chignon rather than loose the way Dan liked it. Worn long, it was far too much of a bother. She unfastened the gold chain with its medallion from around her neck and dropped it into a pocket. It was too heavy, an heirloom piece she wore only on special occasions. She picked up a portfolio of sketches and left the office by the side door. The day was now nothing but a sour taste in her mouth. She would go home to the sanctuary of her house and her faithful Dempsey.

Well, what did you expect? she asked herself as she drove through the changing countryside. *Randall warned you about Dan.* Dan Parker was a man who liked women. He was a lady killer, straight and true. No, not straight and true. A man could not have a girl in every town where he had a job site and be considered straight and true. Out-and-out would do. Dan Parker was an out-and-out womanizer who required a dependable source of feminine comfort in the city where he happened to be working.

She wondered what Dan intended to do with Alicia when his headquarters were moved from Phoenix. Or was she the constant star around which they in the lesser galaxies revolved?

Well, she, Deborah, never intended to find out! *Blast him!* Tears stung her eyes. He had made her aware of something about love that she'd just as soon not have learned. Simply, that if it is painful to be loved, to love involves a greater agony. *Not that I love him. How could I? I don't even know him. Obviously.*

That afternoon Deborah took a break from her drawing board and was in the backyard with Dempsey when she heard a car door slam. The Labrador bounded away to investigate. She ordered her features blank of all expression, furious that her heart had begun to race out of control.

"Hello, you two." Dan's resonant greeting floated across the leaf-strewn lawn.

Chapter Six

Deborah watched Dan open the gate, bend down to scratch Dempsey's ear, then begin the trek toward where she stood unmoving and unsmiling. *He could hurt me*, she thought. *He could hurt me terribly.* He was in khaki slacks, plaid shirt, and Windbreaker, a builder's attire for meeting with contractors and viewing job sites. His stride made short work of the distance, the smile vanishing when it was not met with a response.

"I have a feeling I'm in trouble," he said, pausing with hands on hips in a stance compellingly masculine. Her feigned indifference was almost impossible to maintain in the face of the sudden sharp desire for him.

"I left word at the office to have you call me," she said hollowly, her lips stiff with pain.

"I got it," Dan said, "but I knew I'd better get out here quick after Bea relayed that message Alicia had given you and then told me that you had left early to go home. She said she thought you sounded upset."

"Bea reads too much into things," Deborah said, "and you could have saved yourself a trip. If you had called I would have told you that I've changed my mind about tonight. I'm sorry if that seems to be a habit with me, but I really do have too much work to do. Right now I can't afford a social life, not until the construction documents are finished."

Dan stepped closer, folding large hands around her shoulders. "No, don't pull away, Deborah. Let's talk about Alicia. I can understand what you must be thinking and feeling."

"You don't owe me an explanation, Dan. Your women friends are your business. Silly me to mind the competition, but I do." She shivered beneath his hands. The sun had begun to edge toward the crest of the mountain, and the air was growing colder.

Dan continued quietly. "There's been something too important between us, Deborah. I *do* owe you an explanation about Alicia. I feel you owe me the chance to give you one. Let's go inside. You're getting cold, and I could use a cup of coffee."

Without a word, Deborah led the way to the back door. She had no right to condemn him without a hearing, that was true, but now she was uncomfortable with her feelings for him, no matter what he said about Alicia.

In the kitchen, Dan took off his jacket and straddled a chair to watch Deborah prepare a fresh pot of coffee. His presence seemed to take over the kitchen, affecting her movements, making them self-conscious and clumsy. Always a lonely place for her at twilight, the room would be even lonelier when he was gone.

"Would you believe me," he said, "if I told you that Alicia and I are probably each other's best friend? I haven't had a pal like her since…I lost a buddy of mine a long time ago."

"I've no reason not to believe you about anything, Dan. You just talk, and I'll just listen." The coffee perking, Deborah took a seat at the table.

"I met Alicia when I was about thirty," Dan said. "She had just moved to Phoenix. I was going through a low period in my life, and her sunny disposition was good for me. She was zany and frivolous, game for anything, and she made me laugh and enjoy life again. At first we were lovers, but something rarer developed between us that we hadn't counted on. It was friendship. Sex became a waste of time, utterly pointless. I know that's hard to believe with a woman like her, but it's the truth. We became buddies, there for each other when we were down, sharing the good times when we were up. That's God's honest truth, Deborah. She'd tell you the same thing and *would* if I asked her to."

"That isn't necessary," Deborah said. "It was just that she sounded so…proprietorial, as if you belonged to her."

"Pure press-release talk for the sake of her image in case she was talking to a fan." Dan waved away the comment with a big hand. "She called today to tell me that she's been signed for a new television series. Her career has been on the downswing for a number of years now, so I'm deeply happy for her. She's a deserving lady, a nice one, too. You'd like her."

"I just can't imagine how she would…*could* give you up as…a lover," Deborah said, glancing away, feeling a warm blush spread up her neck.

Dan's gaze sparkled with amusement. He leaned forward, drawing her hand into his. "Thank you. That was a sweet thing to say. But, honey, heart has a lot to do with the quality of lovemaking. Mine was never involved in what went on between Alicia and me. With you, it is. Maybe that's why Alicia and I preferred friendship."

Deborah turned back to him. The eyes shone blue and clear, the eyes of honesty. She wondered what had been the nature of his grief eight years ago. She would have liked to have been there to comfort him, then remembered that at the time she was dealing with her own set of sorrows. She repressed inquiring into it, not only out of tact, but because a disclosure on his part now would call for one on hers later. She pressed his hand and gave him a small, relieved smile. "I'll get that coffee now," she said.

Still, Deborah thought as she poured two steaming cups, her heart now housed a fear that would not let things be as they were. "What is it, Deborah?" Dan asked as he took the cup. "You still look concerned."

"So much has happened to me in the last few days. I've experienced a number of…unsettling feelings. It's not that I mind being unsettled," she said quickly. "Lord knows I can use some shaking up in my existence, but you see, I don't know how much shaking up I can handle. I'm still unsteady from a period in my own life that drained me of the courage to let myself get involved with anyone."

Dan set his coffee cup down. "Tell me about that time, Deborah," he said in quiet earnestness. "Tell me so that I can help and understand you."

But Deborah shook her head. "I'm sorry, Dan. Not now. Maybe never. It's too soon for confidences like that." Only Randall knew of her grief, her shame. *"Dearest child, isn't it time you told me about it?"* he had asked when he found her crying at the bay window one January day when the aspen tree had been as bare as her heart. Estelle Lawson had just died, and Randall's warm concern had been as embracing as a pair of fatherly arms. He had led her to a chair and sat beside her while she poured out the whole story about Roger. And in the next few years when they were all gone—the three people whose lives she had so tragically altered and shortened—he had sat beside her again, gentle and consoling.

Now Deborah said with a small smile, "Thanks for offering anyway."

"A pleasure, believe me." Dan smiled. "So where do we go from here? I know where *I* would like to go, but I don't want to rush my fences with you, Deborah, if that's what you're trying to tell me. I just want to continue seeing you, no bed and board expected, not until you're ready to offer it."

"I just need some time to sort out my feelings and thoughts, Dan. I need some breathing space—"

"How long a breathing space?"

"Give me a week, maybe longer. Both of us have work to do. I've got the architectural drawings to do of the support columns for your headquarters, and I'll be working late at the office on them. They're due to go to our structural engineer next Monday…"

Dan's face fell. The setting sun had made a prism of the glass behind him, firing his hair like a halo and sharply etching the wide breadth of his shoulders. "Damn it, Deborah, you're making too much of this," he complained. "What's the harm of seeing each other if I promise not to carry you off to the bedroom? But okay—" He put up his hand in a placating gesture when he saw that her mind was made up and rose, drawing her into his arms, his blue eyes searching her face. "Have dinner with me anyway," he said. "You look in need of a good meal."

Deborah slipped her arms up around his neck, the feel of him warm and tantalizing and solid. "That bad, huh?"

"Terrible. I don't know how I could bear to kiss you, you looking so washed out and all. But then that's the result of resisting natural urges, so I'm told."

Deborah smiled in amusement, welcoming the descent of his lips.

Later, at her front door, Dan kissed her lengthily again. "Don't—" she said against the hard strength of his neck. "Don't make it hard for me to say good night."

"All right, I won't. Go on in now and get a good night's sleep. Be sure to lock all the doors. I worry about you out here without even an alarm system. Why don't you have one?"

"I do," she said. "I have Dempsey. An alarm system wouldn't get anybody out here in time to prevent a burglary. I have dead-bolt locks on all the doors and windows. Besides, all those alarm gadgets intrude on the aesthetics of the house."

"If you say so, Deborah. I'll call you tomorrow from Josie's because I plan to be at the site all day. Okay?"

"Okay." She smiled, lifting her lips for his kiss, dreading his leaving.

Dan waited until he heard the click of the front door lock before getting into his car, then cursed under his breath. *Damn that Alicia! She'd nearly ruined everything!*

In a wave of loneliness, Deborah listened to Dan's car pulling away. She'd shown good judgment, she convinced herself, in keeping him at a distance for a while. Although Dan was honest and sincere, he owed her nothing. She could very well be only a temporary diversion. She had to have time to answer Randall's emotionally provocative question: "Can you afford to be hurt again?"

She did not know. In the last eight years she'd tried to reduce the risk of being loved. She was unfamiliar, totally, with the other side of the coin, the risk of loving. But today, for those few hours in which she had been unable to work, to concentrate, to think of anything but Dan, she had glimpsed what that was like. To love and then to be discarded…undoubtedly many women in Dan's life had suffered that experience. Was she whole enough, had the seams knit strongly enough to risk what loving Dan might mean? Could she endure another abandonment?

Deborah put Dempsey outside while she went upstairs to get ready for bed. And then, of course, she thought as she pulled back covers and set the alarm, there was the other problem that must be dealt with even if their course was smooth. How would Dan react when she told him about what had happened eight years ago?

As if her sentence had been delivered only yesterday, Deborah could clearly hear Estelle's words: "I just want you to know, Deborah, that for the rest of my life I shall hold you responsible for the death of my son." And Estelle had held to that until death, which had followed shortly after Roger's. It was as if he had been the sun of her existence; once it had set, night had fallen quickly for the aging matriarch. The pictures of the car accident that had claimed Roger's life had never dimmed in Deborah's memory. Estelle, wishing to hurt, had sent them along with newspaper reports of the tragedy. One line had haunted Deborah for years: "Those who arrived to attend Roger Lawson's wedding stayed to attend his funeral."

Her parents never forgave her for the grief she had caused. In addition to everything else, she had destroyed a friendship of fifty years. Estelle refused to see Isabelle, to listen to any pleas or apologies, to grant any forgiveness. Isabelle, her spirit broken by the social stigma as well as the shame of Deborah's action, could hardly bring herself to speak to her only child. Caught between the two women he loved, Ben shrank into himself, shuffling through the days of discord with an air of perpetual bewilderment.

Her parents had seen her move to Denver as a desertion. Deborah should stay in Savannah and suffer with them the shame of what she had done. She might have submitted to their demands had she not been convinced that Roger would have wanted her to go to Denver. He would have wanted her to try her wings, to fly away. One morning she was standing at the window of her bedroom, the untroubled spring day like a reproach to her heart. "Roger," she had said, making up her mind, "I'm going to Denver. If I don't go, not one good thing will have come from all this." There had followed a strange, ephemeral few minutes, possibly imagined, but incredibly comforting. Over her had flowed a sensation of warmth, of light. A great peace descended. She had stood very still, her eyes filling, and she had whispered, "Thank you, Roger."

In a nightgown and robe, Deborah, burdened with the heavy weight of memories, went downstairs to the back door to call Dempsey. He seemed interested in something in the alley beyond the fence. Was there a car parked out there in the shadow of the mountain? She could make out only Dempsey's dark shape. She called him sharply, and he responded at once. *Nothing is out there,* she scolded herself. Dempsey would have set up a howl. Dan's worry about locked doors and burglars had her seeing things.

The next morning, Deborah was at her drawing board early, hoping for a head start on the columns before being bombarded with questions. The intercom buzzed. She pushed it with a sigh and Bea asked, "Deborah, may I speak with you?"

"Shoot," she said.

"Not over the phone. I'll be around in a few minutes."

It meant a delay, but Bea had sounded concerned. The secretary's usually unflappable demeanor was missing when she came into Deborah's office moments later. "It looks serious," Deborah said, asking Bea to sit down. "What's the matter?"

"I think I owe you an apology."

Deborah's brows rose. "You do? What for?"

"For tattling on you to Randall about leaving Josie's with Dan Parker the other night. I had no idea he would get so upset about it. You know I adore him, Deborah, but honestly, the dear man lives in the *Victorian* era. He's a walking antique."

"I'd say that's an apt description." Deborah smiled. "He means well, though."

"That he does, dear, but when he mentioned that he'd spoken to you about leaving with Mr. Parker, I nearly died. I told Randall because I was so happy about it. I think Mr. Parker would be a wonderful match for you. He's rich, successful, good looking. I thought Randall would be happy, too, but no, he flew into one of those rare, quiet rages of his that are far more frightening than the kind where people throw things. And then yesterday, when Alicia Dameron called, I didn't know that she and Mr. Parker had once been a hot item, not until Randall told me. I thought she'd called on business."

"You told Randall that Alicia Dameron had called?"

"Well, yes, dear. I was so excited about talking to her and mentioned it when I went in to tell him that you'd left. I've been mad at myself for putting her through to you ever since."

"Well, don't be," Deborah said, "and you don't owe me an apology about anything. I certainly didn't think you had tattled on me. Randall is just looking out for my welfare. He's not as sold on Dan as you are."

"Obviously," said Bea wryly. "Randall is seldom wrong about people, but he surely must be about Mr. Parker. The man is so forthright."

"Isn't he?" Deborah smiled tenderly.

In the afternoon, Deborah had another visitor. "What brings you to this neck of the woods, as if I didn't know?" Deborah said, switching off the high-intensity light above the drawing board and spinning around on the stool to give Randall her full attention.

"Was I or was I not right about Alicia Dameron?" he asked with satisfaction, regarding her closely.

Deborah deliberated a moment. "What, just exactly, do you mean?"

"Don't hedge with me, Deborah," Randall snapped. "Bea told me that the woman called here yesterday for Dan and spoke with you. And don't tell me to mind my own business because I won't." He puffed fiercely on his pipe.

"So I see," said Deborah. "Randall, if you're asking me whether or not Alicia is in Dan's life still, then the answer is yes."

"Aha! How do you feel about that?"

"Jealous."

"Good. Now maybe you will come to your senses. You're not planning to continue seeing him, are you?"

"Not for a while. I need some breathing room."

"Very wise. Have you thought at all about what I said concerning the will?"

"No, I haven't."

"Somehow that does not surprise me." He peered over her shoulder at the drawing. "Looking good," he said. "When will you be through?"

"Probably never if these interruptions don't stop," she said pointedly. "I may have to work on the columns over the weekend."

"Well, I must say," he said, his glance roving over her face, inspecting it, "a good night's sleep does wonders for you. You look very rested."

"How do you know that I had a good night's sleep?" Deborah asked in surprise.

Randall was on his way out. At the door he turned to her with a smile. "The power of my observation, my dear. It is never wrong."

In the early afternoon, Dan telephoned. All day she had missed him. The memory of him hung over her like the aromatic scent of Randall's pipe. As she worked on the stately columns that would support the seven floors of his headquarters, she thought about

91

the reputation he had earned as a builder and developer. Was he really interested only in making money? Were women merely restorative pastimes outside business hours?

She could not disguise her delight when she heard his voice. "How nice," she said, smiling into the receiver. "Are you in Josie's?"

"Uh-huh. I'm having a beer and missing you. Could I talk you into seeing me tonight?"

"You could, but I'm hoping you won't try. You promised not to rush your fences, remember?"

"I remember," he grumbled. "Okay, so what about Saturday? You'll need a break from that drawing board by then. I want to spend the whole day with you. Do you mind?"

"Would you be willing to do anything I suggested, put yourself in my hands for the entire day?"

"The entire night, too, if you like," Dan offered.

"Dan!" She gasped, surprising herself. "Not over the phone! Anybody could be listening!" She sounded as dramatic as Bea but some instinct warned her that the office was no longer a safe place for private telephone conversations with Dan.

The bantering tone faded. "Are you serious, Deborah? Who would want to listen in on our conversations?"

A romance-starved secretary, a boss who thinks your intentions dishonorable, a jealous and spiteful colleague out to discredit me—these were the choices she could have mentioned. "What would you say to driving up toward Arapaho National Forest to see the trees and have a picnic?"

"Anything you say. If you'll get the food together, I'll bring the wine. Dinner is on me. And let's take Dempsey with us."

"Oh, he'll like that!" Deborah said eagerly. "Will nine o'clock be too early?"

"Not to be with you, Deborah."

*   *   *

Deborah was ready by the time Dan arrived at the kitchen door Saturday morning. The windows and inner door were open to allow in the sunshine and fresh air carrying a nip of the frost that had fallen during the night. Dempsey, sensing preparations afoot for an outing when his mistress took down the picnic basket, had stayed close to her heels all morning. "We're going to the mountains today, Demps," she told him, packing sausage, deviled eggs, French bread, apples, an assortment of cheeses, and the pièce de resistance, a chocolate cake baked the night before.

"Hello, there!" Dan called through the outer glass door, stamping leaves from his boots. Dempsey barked to alert her of his presence and together they went to welcome him. He had already been on his morning run, she could tell, for his cheeks still held the ruddy glow of healthy exertion. Their eyes exchanged a laugh through the glass.

"Good morning," she returned, unlocking it and backing up to allow him room. He entered the kitchen, bringing in a surge of the outdoors and the ebullience of high spirits. His eyes were as clear as a fine, bright sky.

"I've missed you," he said, his sweeping glance taking her in all at once.

"Likewise," Deborah said, suddenly a little shy, hesitant, holding fast to the reins of her feelings.

Dan understood. "Come here." He grinned, the laughter coming from deep within his chest. She was all at once enveloped by his down-filled jacket, drawn into its warm depths where her arms slipped readily around a lean, firm waist. Slowly, his mouth settled over hers, and for a long, bliss-filled moment she was cocooned in a sensual fusion of warmth and flannel and hard, muscular flesh.

LEILA MEACHAM

"I thought you were too busy a man for this sort of thing," Deborah murmured when her mouth was freed.

"What—kissing you or going on a picnic?"

"Both. It's a package deal."

"I'll take it," he said. "Wrap it up."

She could not joke about it, she found, as her throat tightened. "How about some coffee while we load?" she suggested.

There was no point in taking his rental car. Dan could drive hers, she offered. A short while later, with Dempsey ensconced on the backseat, they began the journey west, and Deborah relaxed to enjoy the sensation of the Colorado Rockies in autumn. Beginning in mid-September and running through October, she told Dan, the Rocky Mountain range had to be the most spectacular sight on earth. "Starting with the aspen groves, trees at the highest elevations change color first, but as the season progresses, the colors spread down the mountains, like bright paint dripping down a green canvas," she explained, "until they finally reach the foothills."

Her companion looked across at her, observing the excitement in the amber eyes, themselves reminding him of the splendor of a bright fall day. "You're really sold on Colorado, aren't you?"

"I don't think I could be happy anywhere else. I adore mountains. They're so solid and enduring."

"Tell me about your parents," he said suddenly. "Are they still living?"

"No," she said, startled at the question. "They died within the first four years of my coming to Denver."

"I'm sorry," Dan said, glancing quickly at her profile. "Do you ever go back to Savannah?"

"No. There's no reason to. No relatives are left. When my parents died, I sold the house, the place where I grew up."

94

Dan smiled. "What about your friends? Do you ever have the desire to go back to see them?"

"Occasionally, but I never have." Sometimes, she wanted to tell him, she missed Savannah terribly. It would have been wonderful to go home, back to Pecan Street, to the house where she was born, to the neighborhood and the friends she had known since childhood. But she was no longer welcome there. She was known as the girl who had jilted a fine man on the eve of her wedding, provoked his death, and caused her parents to grieve themselves into early graves.

Deborah said, "I don't want you to think that Savannah isn't dear to me. It's a lovely old Southern city, but I felt stifled there, as if I were mildewing in a hope chest with great-grand-mother's lace tablecloth. I had to break free of it, go somewhere where I could breathe and live my own life without answering to anybody."

"And have you been able to do that?"

"Yes," she said. "Now I don't have anybody to answer to, nobody at all."

Around noon, Deborah directed Dan north from the interstate onto a two-lane highway leading into the deep, brilliant world of the Arapaho National Forest. Dan let out an awed exclamation. "It's something, isn't it?" Deborah breathed, experiencing the usual seasonal frustration of trying to assimilate so much beauty all at once. In the moving car, with the brilliant reds and rusts and greens and yellows flashing by on either side, she had the sensation of suddenly being plunged into a universe composed only of silence and dazzling color. Even Dempsey seemed awed by the majestic grandeur.

"This road," Deborah explained in a tone full of respect for the splendor, "leads to Eldorado Canyon. There's a bluff we'll come to in a few minutes that you can see from the road. We can turn off there, and it's just a short distance to a clearing. I found it when I first came to Colorado. I've come back many times."

"By yourself?" Dan asked, looking at her.

"No," she said. "With Dempsey."

Deborah suggested they wait to unpack the car until after their exploration of the forest. "The chipmunks and camp robbers can make quick work of a picnic basket," she said. "They won't bother us when we get back because of Dempsey."

"Camp robbers?" he asked.

"Birds." She laughed. "Don't you know anything about this business of picnicking in Colorado?"

For answer, he tweaked her nose. Once out of the car, Dan held out his hand and she slipped hers into it. For a moment they stood in awed silence, letting the forest reach their deepest senses. Dempsey had already bounded off in pursuit of a tuft-eared squirrel.

"I feel like whispering," Dan whispered.

"You should. It's nature's cathedral."

They began the climb toward the bluff, pausing to admire the aspens growing along the slope.

She asked if he knew why the aspens quake. No, he did not, he said, but he had a feeling he was about to be enlightened.

"Indeed you are," Deborah assured him. "Ute legend has it that at one time, when all living things trembled in anticipation of the Great Spirit's arrival on earth, the aspen stood still, showing irreverence. That did not set too well with the Great Spirit. So, as a penance, the aspen was sentenced to quake forever."

Deborah finished the recital as they came to a break in the trees, suffused with sunlight. An aspen tree, golden with light, quivered in front of them, and Deborah went to hold a mass of the fluttering leaves loosely in her hands. Dan came to stand beside her, fascinated by the gentleness with which she held the trembling leaves. Unexpectedly, she said, "Not to be forgiven is a terrible thing."

They explored and hiked for over an hour until Dan announced that he was hungry. Deborah discovered that she was eager for his reaction to the meal. "Let's go see if we can find anything to eat," she said mysteriously.

His expression of pleasure when the food was laid out more than satisfied her desire to please. He had set the folding table and chairs in a stream of sunlight that felt pleasant in the chill of the forest. They ate and drank slowly, savoring the wine, the peace, the quiet, each other. Deborah, mindful of the vault of the sky, the floor like gold beneath their feet, the leaves twinkling their approval when Dan's laughter rang through the trees, had never known such a time of utter contentment. She wished she could capture the moment forever and then realized that perhaps she had. Never again would she enter a forest without the memory of this day with Dan.

"I...baked a cake last night," Deborah said at the meal's end, suddenly overcome with the peculiar shyness that sometimes struck during certain moments with Dan. "The recipe is one that my mother especially prized. She refused to give it to anyone, or if she did she altered it so that no one else's ever tasted as good as hers. It was my favorite dessert as a child. I thought you might like it, too."

She was conscious of Dan regarding her in rather stunned surprise. "You baked a cake for me?" he asked quietly. "I feel highly complimented, Deborah. No one has ever done that for me."

"I hope you like it," she said, lifting out the rich chocolate cake. She cut him a generous slice, then bent to give Dempsey a treat while Dan ate the first bite, afraid to watch his face.

"It's delicious," he pronounced. "More than delicious. Sensational. It will become my favorite, too."

97

The statement implied a long association with her and her mother's recipe. Deborah did not pursue the point. It was enough that he had said it.

She didn't want the outing to end. While Dan packed the car, she went back to the stream of sunlight for one final memory. "What are you thinking?" he called to her. He was beside the car, jacket open, hair ruffled, a portion of chest exposed at the neck of the plaid shirt, legs powerful in the taut jeans.

"How well-suited to mountains you are," she answered.

Chapter Seven

It was Dan who first saw the wide-open front door. The mountain's late afternoon shadow had fallen across the circular drive, and Deborah was occupied with keeping Dempsey's curious nose out of the grocery sack containing steaks for dinner. "Stay in the car, Deborah, and lock the doors after me," Dan ordered quietly as he stopped the car. "I want Dempsey to come with me."

"What's the matter?" she asked, alarmed by the quiet urgency in his voice. Then, over Dan's shoulder, she saw the open door. "Oh, no!"

"Stay put," he said again. "Keep the motor running. Come on, Dempsey."

"Dan, you can't go in there! Somebody may still be inside!"

"I don't think so. There's no vehicle about, not unless it's in the alley. In which case the front door wouldn't be open to warn you of a burglar inside. I'll check the back first. Get behind the wheel and be ready to move if you have to."

"Dan—"

"Do as I ask, Deborah."

She watched as Dan and the dog disappeared around the corner of the house, her throat nearly closed in fear. She knew that she had locked the front door as she left. Dan had watched her. They should simply leave now and go somewhere to call the police. What if the burglars were still in the house and should hurt Dan!

Deborah was ready to go to his aid when Dan appeared in the open doorway. His face had the look of granite. "You were lucky," he said grimly. "They broke a kitchen window to get in, but at least they didn't damage the house. It's safe to come in. I'll call the sheriff's office."

While Dan telephoned, Deborah took a survey of the house, sickened by the fact that the sanctity of her home had been violated. But at least the man—why did she think there had been only one?—had not wreaked havoc with her precious furnishings, the china, crystal, and art objects inherited from her parents. He had taken all the sterling, a mink coat that had belonged to her mother, the pearl and diamond earrings she had worn Saturday night with Dan, and the gold chain with the medallion. Her other jewelry was still locked in the safe. She was missing radios and cameras, a tape recorder, and the small television set that had been in the kitchen. Oddly, the thief had also taken a few books and other personal things, including a framed picture of herself.

But in the workroom off the kitchen, she made a terrible discovery. "Dan!" she cried out to him in the kitchen, where he had been speaking on the phone. "He took the architectural drawings!" Frantically she searched her mind for where else they could be, but no, she remembered working on them here last night while waiting for the cake to bake.

"Architectural drawings of the project?" Dan entered the small studio with a frown. "Are you sure?"

"Yes," she said, her face suddenly gone white. "They were of the support columns and—and I had completed several others—"

"But there must be copies at the office?"

"No," she said, fighting down a surge of hysteria. "I've been working on them here at night because I was falling behind at the office. I couldn't work without interruption." Her eyes widened at the look on his face. "Dan," she offered quickly, hoping to head off his anger, "I can redraw the columns. By tacking a few hours onto my workday and working weekends, I can make up for the lost time."

Dan's healthy tan had taken on the color of a forbidding winter twilight. The dark brows drew together as he approached. "Exactly what are we talking about here? How long did it take you to do the drawings?"

"A week." Deborah swallowed.

"A week! We don't have an extra week, Deborah!"

"Dan, you've got to trust me. I can redraw them. I promise you they'll be ready by the twenty-second."

"How? By driving yourself into the ground? Not eating or sleeping? What kind of answer is that to this problem?"

"That's my concern. I've been under pressure before, but I've always come through. You said yourself that I'm known around town as a lady who keeps deadlines."

"You were foolish to keep those drawings here, Deborah, especially since I've told you a number of times that this house is a sitting target for vandals."

"Yes," she conceded, moistening dry lips. "I—it just never entered my mind that a thief would take something as useless to him as a set of architectural drawings." She looked at him remorsefully. "I'm so sorry, Dan."

It was on the tip of his tongue to reply that her apology wouldn't mean a tinker's damn to the others whose fortunes and livelihoods were riding on this project. It certainly wouldn't to him if he had to renegotiate his financial arrangements at a higher interest rate because the documents weren't ready by the deadline.

But her expression was terrified. Not a trace remained of the earlier vibrant glow that had been on her face. It occurred to him that she might be worried about more than just the deadline. She could be afraid that the situation might jeopardize their relationship. He took her by the shoulders. "Let's not slay any dragons until we see 'em," he said reasonably, controlling his ire. "Time enough to worry about the deadline if and when it's not met. I have every confidence it will be. Now come on." He smoothed back her hair. "Let's get some color back into that face. This isn't the end of the world, and I'm not some Great Spirit condemning you to quake forever."

She smiled slightly. "You would have every right to."

"Try me when and if you don't make the deadline."

"No thanks. I believe I'll pass on that."

He kissed her forehead. "What you need to do now is make a list of the items stolen. The sheriff will want one. After I unload the car, I'll board up that broken window. Do you have any lumber lying around?"

"In the garage, left over from when the house was built," Deborah answered.

It was the young deputy's opinion that she had been robbed by an amateur. "The evidence supports that theory, Miss Standridge. The burglar took items at random, some worthless to him, such as your picture and those drawings, and left other things that he could have sold for a pretty penny if he'd known their value. The way he entered the house, by breaking the window instead of cutting it, smacks of someone who was just passing by, some bold kid maybe, who went up and rang your doorbell. When nobody answered and the dog didn't bark, he knew you weren't home. He went around to the back, knocked in that window, unlatched it, came in, and took what he wanted." He gave her a look of sympathy. "I know it's a small blessing, but be grateful that he didn't make a mess of things. So many of them do, just out of spite."

"There's no hope of recovering my things, I suppose?"

"I wish I could say there was, ma'am. We'll sure call you if anything on that list turns up. In the meantime, I suggest you secure your home a little better."

"Burglar bars, you think?" asked Dan.

"They won't stop a professional, but they will a casual thief like this one."

Dan walked with the deputy to his car, where they conversed for a few minutes. When he returned, he found Deborah unloading the picnic basket, her movements quiet and composed. He observed her in silence, reminded of how differently the day had begun. Since their conversation in the workroom, they had spoken only a few words to each other. "Would you like a drink?" he asked. "I could certainly use one."

She nodded, and he returned shortly with a Tom Collins. She was putting the steaks, still in the grocery sack, into the refrigerator. "Don't forget those when you leave," she said. "I may forget to remind you."

"I thought we were grilling them for dinner."

"I'd rather not, if you don't mind, Dan. I'd like to get started on the drawings, and frankly, I'd like to be alone this evening."

Dan drew closer, his brow furrowing. "It's not a good idea for you to be alone tonight, Deborah. And I certainly don't think you should work on the drawings. You could make a mistake, and we can certainly do without those."

She faced him squarely. "Mr. Parker, I do not make mistakes on architectural drawings."

"Deborah, if you're worried that this is going to have any

affect on us, you can lay that worry aside. One of the problems in working with women in business," he sighed, "is that you people cannot separate personal and business feelings. This problem today affects our *business* relationship, not us personally, understand?"

"I'll give it some thought," she said.

"Good. Now, I'm staying for dinner. If I leave, you won't eat. Also I'm staying the night, unless you think you can throw me out bodily."

To the sound of hammer striking nails, Deborah washed the plastic cups and plates and restored the picnic basket to order, her mind on what Dan had said. She wished she could believe him, but it had been her experience that failure always affected love. Love withdrew in the face of failure. She should know. Withdrawal of affection, or the threat of it, had been her parents' punishment for failure. That dark source of emotion had given birth to the excruciating headaches that had plagued most of her life. One was gathering force now behind her temples. She had not been bothered with them in recent years, not since working for Randall Hayden.

She fed Dempsey and set the table in the dining room, opening the silverware drawer without thinking. She could not have said why she began to cry when she saw again the empty velvet compartments. Possessions were, after all, only possessions. But not hers. They were memories, all that were left of the years in Savannah, of her parents and the house on Pecan Street—the only tangible comfort in her banishment from the dear and familiar. She had designed this house for them in the peace of the foothills, the shelter of the mountain, and now she knew how much they meant to her and how easily they could be taken away.

Dempsey, disturbed by the sight of his mistress in tears, sat on his haunches and whimpered in distress. "It's all right, boy," said Dan, coming up behind them. "I'll take over now."

Dan lay awake in the guest room, propped high on pillows and thinking. The evening had not been rescued. Deborah had not stayed long in his arms when he found her crying but had dried her eyes quickly and gone about the preparations for dinner. After a silent meal, she had left him to the television set and gone into the studio, closing the door. Without her, he had not wanted to watch television, not with a briefcase of work waiting in the trunk of his car.

At the kitchen table, facing the closed door of the studio, he had been unable to concentrate on the papers spread out for his attention. He kept seeing Deborah in the stream of sunlight those last few minutes in the forest, heard again her words, re-experienced the feeling that had swept over him.

Damn! He had not meant to upbraid the beautiful woman in the forest. Why couldn't she understand that? The builder had been angry with the architect handling the most important project of his career. Finding her crying, it had been the man who had taken her into his arms, sensitive to the pain of a woman hurting from the violation of her home.

He thought he had been unusually understanding, but Deborah had withdrawn from him, gone into some sort of shell as if she didn't quite trust him. Apprehension fluttered in his chest. Had she slipped away from him forever? He would not allow it. He must find her and bring her back in the only way he knew how. He had planned too long, too carefully, to lose her now. Tossing back the covers, he slipped into a robe kept packed for emergency trips. He had gone out to his car to get the bag after Deborah had retired, not wanting her to think he had come prepared to spend the night.

Dan opened the door of Deborah's bedroom softly, standing

framed in the doorway for the benefit of Dempsey. Instantly he saw the outline of two alert ears, then the muscular rippling of the big body as the Labrador ambled around the corner of the bed to confirm Dan's identity. "Come on downstairs with me, boy," Dan whispered.

After shutting Dempsey in the kitchen, once more Dan climbed the stairs and entered Deborah's bedroom. Starlight bathed the room and her sleeping form with a luminescent glow. As he approached the bed, his eye fell upon a prescription bottle on the bedside table. He picked it up and examined the label, recognizing the name Midrin. He knew the capsules were prescribed for migraines. He had picked up countless bottles of the medication from the pharmacy for his father, who had suffered from them for years before he died. Glancing down at Deborah, his heart moved in pity. Now he understood the nature of her paleness, the faint discoloration he had noticed beneath her eyes as she bid him good night. She had been in the racking throes of a migraine. Maybe it had also been responsible for her remoteness, the detachment with which she had regarded him for the rest of the evening. Maybe she had not gone away from him at all. He leaned over to pull the covers up to her chin.

Deborah, accustomed to a mantle of starshine, sensed the change in the light above her and stirred in her sleep. Dan drew up. Heavily, her lids fluttered open. "Dan?" she whispered, wondering sleepily if the tall man beside her bed were part of the dream from which she was emerging.

"Go back to sleep," he urged. "I'm sorry I disturbed you."

"Why are you here?"

"I...was worried about you. You seemed so distant all evening. I wanted to bring you back from wherever you had gone." He nodded toward the prescription bottle. "Why didn't you tell me you were suffering from a migraine."

"It's my problem."

"I want to share your problems."

"I gave you one this afternoon."

"That's not what I mean, Deborah, and you know it."

She held out her hand and he took it. "Stay with me," she asked.

"Only to hold you, Deborah. You need your rest."

"I need you."

He removed his robe, climbed in beside her, and gathered her to him. Her flannel-gowned body was warm and soft against his bare skin. "And I, you," he said.

Because she had not wanted to spoil his weekend, Deborah waited until Monday morning to tell Randall about the theft. His expression registered quiet shock. "I am more concerned for you, Deborah. Are you all right? Where did you stay the last two nights? Surely not in a house with a broken window?"

"Dan boarded the window for me, Randall, which made the house quite safe, and of course, I had Dempsey." She had hoped to avoid mentioning Dan in the narration of the robbery.

Randall looked put out. "You called for Dan's help rather than mine?"

Deborah sighed. "I was with him Saturday, Randall. We went on a picnic. Under the circumstances, I'm grateful he was with me."

"Yes," Randall agreed, "thank goodness someone besides Dempsey was with you. What was Dan's reaction when you discovered the drawings were missing?"

Deborah hesitated. Was he asking on behalf of the firm? Or was he curious about Dan's reactions when his business interests were thwarted? "He was surprisingly understanding," Deborah answered. "He could have really raked me over the coals about

107

having the drawings at the house rather than here under lock and key. He had already expressed concern about the security of the house."

"I see…" Randall said slowly, eyeing her as if he did not quite believe her. "What does this do to the deadline?"

"We can still make it," she said emphatically.

Her mentor looked at his watch. "Let's talk about it in the meeting. The others are already assembled."

In the conference room, news of the theft was met with a variety of responses. John Turner leaned back and crossed his arms. "So that means we're behind the power curve, doesn't it? Looks like I'll be working from your preliminary designs after all, Deborah." There was just the slightest trace of smugness in his tone.

"No," Deborah said, avoiding looking at Randall. This was one time she might not get his support. "I still want you to wait for my architectural details before you do the structural calculations."

John stared at her, his mouth open slightly. "You're being bullheaded. "I've already calculated the loads for the second floor. Now I need to get to work on the computations for those columns." He turned to the arbitrator of his disputes with Deborah. "Randall, help me out on this. I need to get started or I could fall behind in my own schedule."

"Deborah, I appreciate the fact that those columns are the focal point of your design for the headquarters building, but time does not permit us to wait for you to finish your drawings before John can begin his calculations," Randall said.

Deborah looked beseechingly at the engineer. "John, I'll get them to you in one week. By working at night and next weekend, I can get them to you first thing Monday morning. You have other support structures to work on in the meantime, as you well know."

"Won't that interfere with your social life, Deb?" asked Tony Pierson, grinning.

"Her social life was the cause of all this," John commented dryly.

"Oh, John—" Tony admonished, supported by a murmur of protests from around the table.

"Boys and girls!" Randall's rebuke had the effect of a teacher rapping on a desk. "This bickering must stop. John, I must ask you to refrain from inciting this kind of discussion in the future. Do you understand?"

"Yes sir," said John, two dull red spots burning beneath the sallow surface of his cheeks.

"Deborah," Randall said with a sigh, "let's compromise on this. If in two days you see that you're not going to have your drawings ready for John within a week, then he's to use your renderings. Agreed?"

"Agreed," said Deborah.

"John?"

"Agreed," said John shortly.

"All right, that's settled. Now a word of caution to all of you: Since you'll be working down to the very last minute of the deadline, there will not be time for the documents to go through an in-house quality control check," he warned, referring to the department whose duty it was to check for detail and dimensional errors before plans were issued for a building permit. "You must check and double-check every figure, every detail, every dimension. That's it for this morning." He smiled mellowly.

Deborah was hard at work with T-square and triangle when a call came through from Dan. "Can we meet somewhere for lunch?" he asked.

"Oh, dear, Dan, I don't know. We have so much to do here. I'd planned to work through lunch."

"I have to see you, Deborah. Something has come up that I don't want to discuss over the phone."

"Let me meet you somewhere for a half hour or so, but not for lunch." *And not at the office either*, she wanted to say.

Dan seemed to have sensed her thought. "Whatever you say. Name a place."

"Glendale Park is about two blocks from the office. How about there?" she suggested. The day was too beautiful to spend all of it inside, and she needed to unwind a bit.

"Sold," he said.

Dan was waiting for her at a picnic table in the deserted park when she arrived. He got up and walked toward her, tall and elegant and masculine in a camel's hair sport coat and sharply creased trousers. Her heart began to pound—would it never beat normally at the sight of him? "You look a little tired," Dan said after they had kissed. "I should have let you sleep." He rubbed a soothing thumb beneath her eye.

"You were better than sleep," she assured him. "I'm not tired, just showing the strain of the office. The atmosphere is a little tense today."

"Was Randall upset with you about the drawings?"

"Randall is never upset with me about anything," she said, taking his arm.

"Unlike me?" Dan's large hand folded over hers in the crook of his arm.

Deborah did not want to go into that. "That's over now. What did you want to discuss with me?" They walked in ankle-deep leaves toward the picnic table. It was the last day of September; soon the trees would be stretching bare arms to an indifferent sky.

110

"I have to go back to Phoenix for a while. Work is piling up to such an extent that my secretary thinks she's being buried alive. For the time being, I've done all that I can do here."

Her throat felt dry suddenly. "Of course," she said. "When will you be leaving?"

"I have an afternoon flight out. I know it seems sudden, but something has come up that requires my immediate attention. Will you be all right?" Dan gave her a worried look as they sat down. "Feel free to use the town house if you're uneasy about staying out in the foothills. I can leave you a key."

"No." She tried to smile easily. "Thanks just the same, but I won't be driven out of my home. Dempsey is all the protection I need. Actually, it's just as well you're returning to Phoenix now. I will be working late at the office every night and on weekends. We really couldn't see each other."

Dan took her chin between his thumb and finger, turning her to look at him. "I am going to miss you, honey. And I'll be back as soon as I can, probably in three weeks. Oh, by the way—" He patted his jacket pockets, taking from one a memo slip on which were printed several telephone numbers. He indicated one with his thumb. "This number belongs to a security systems firm. It installs burglar bars. I know you don't like the idea of them, Deborah, but you really should get them installed on your windows. I arranged for a company representative to come out on Saturday morning and talk to you about them unless you call and instruct otherwise. These are the phone numbers of my office and house. Call if you need anything or if you get lonesome."

Deborah took the piece of paper. "Thank you for taking the time to do this for me and for coming to tell me that you're leaving. It's been a busy morning for you, I know." She was succeeding in keeping her voice even, preventing it from giving away her feelings. She would not be clingy. She wondered if Dan would be seeing Alicia when he returned to Phoenix.

"I seem to enjoy making time for you, Deborah. It's a new experience for me, making time for a woman. Did you know that leaves have caught in your hair?" He removed one and held it close to her face. "They match your eyes," he said in wonder.

Returning to the office, Deborah forced herself to get down to work again, but the sun had gone from the day and a fog of depression settled in. Three weeks. Three whole weeks, maybe more, before she would hear that deep voice, see those broad shoulders, feel his arms around her again. The buzz of the intercom broke into her wistfulness. It was a phone call from Dan. "I have five minutes to catch my plane," he said, "but I couldn't remember if I told you that I'll miss you."

Deborah smiled, her heart lifting. She could imagine him, too big for the phone booth, one leg crossed over the other, leather briefcase at his feet, silver-gray hair gleaming—an American success story in his custom-tailored coat. "Several times." She laughed. "But I might have forgotten if you hadn't called."

"See that you remember." A pause followed, as if he had forgotten something, then he said carelessly, as if he had not, "See you soon, honey."

Just before five o'clock, Deborah was summoned to Randall's office. He was carefully watering the luxuriant assortment of plants aesthetically arranged around the room. Randall tended well whatever he possessed, Deborah granted, warmed by affection for the now rather fragile figure bent over a brass container of flowering gloxinias. Whatever he cared for thrived. The longevity of his plants was legendary, and until last year, he'd had a Sheltie that had lived to twenty years of age. Under his care, the firm had flourished like his plants, but now a shadow had fallen over it. Deborah could feel its presence like a dark presentiment.

"You wanted to see me," she said gently.

"Yes, dear child. Bea and I are going to the Ship Tavern for dinner. They're featuring Kakanee salmon this evening. How about joining us?"

"I'd love to," she said immediately, grateful that she would not have to go directly home to face the first of many long evenings without Dan. "It's sweet of you to include me."

"It's been too long since the three of us dined together at the Tavern."

"It will be like old times."

"Not quite, my dear, not quite." With a small pair of scissors Randall clipped off a discolored leaf of the gloxinia. After a small silence, he said, "The years have rewarded my faith in you, Deborah. Today when I look at the examples of your work, what they have contributed to the firm's growth and reputation, I feel quite like the investor who bought the first original shares of IBM. We probably share a similar pride in our foresight and wisdom, in the success of our discoveries. We'll leave from here right after work."

Designed around a collection of models from America's clipper ship past, the Ship Tavern in Denver's historical Brown Palace Hotel was one of the few restaurants—or public rooms, as Randall preferred to call it—that could live up to his Victorian view of graciousness.

"I do so love this place," Bea said as they were shown to one of the checkered-clothed tables. "I'm glad you could join us, Deborah."

"I am assuming the reason we have the pleasure of your company tonight is because Mr. Parker took himself back to

Phoenix," Randall said. "I can't say that I'm surprised. He realized that in order for you to finish those drawings on time, he would have to stop distracting you."

Deborah's heart stood still. Was that why Dan had gone back to Phoenix—to insure that she finish the drawings on time? The thought had not occurred to her. "How did you know that Dan had returned to Phoenix?" she asked Randall, striving for a casual tone.

"He called to inform me. It was merely a courtesy since I am sure he had already told you of his plans." His blue eyes were mild as they perused the wine list.

On the surface, the evening was reminiscent of many such evenings in the past. Randall ordered Champagne, and they chatted familiarly while waiting for the delicately flavored Colorado salmon. But for Deborah, the evening had lost its blush. Randall had raised a doubt about Dan's real reason for returning to Phoenix. Had he wanted to get out of her hair until the drawings were completed? In Denver he would have to see her; in Phoenix he would have an excuse not to. She couldn't blame him if that were so, of course. The project was all important right now. The two of them could wait. But still...

It was after midnight when she turned off the bright light over her drawing board in the studio. Dan had called earlier, and his deep voice still vibrated in her mind, in her heart. How she missed him! She could think of nothing else as she worked. He had sounded tired and wistful. "I'm going to bed now to dream of you," he had said. "I miss you, honey."

But neither sleep nor dreams would come for Deborah. Something was disturbing her, some vague, formless something left over from the day—a comment, a gesture, an expression—that she should see, make some sense of, but could not. Whatever it was nagged at her, like an unidentifiable sound in a familiar place. Did it have to do with the real reason Dan had returned to Phoenix? She thought not. She had decided to lay that doubt aside and believe Dan. Finally a possibility suggested itself. She had forgotten about the car she thought she had seen in the alley last week. Could that have been the burglar watching her house? That had to be it. That was the origin of her worry. She would install a more powerful light on the back porch.

That settled, Deborah waited for sleep to come. Moments ticked by. She realized that she had not located the real source of the trouble. The sound was still there.

Chapter Eight

Snow had fallen almost continuously for a week. From the bay window, Deborah watched the soft, gentle flakes drift to the deeply blanketed ground and catch in the heavily weighted branches of the aspen tree. It was the kind of snow that meant money in the bank for the ski resorts, but for her it symbolized another day of sameness in a white, changeless landscape. She turned from the window with a sigh. It was so miserable to miss someone in winter. There was no escape from cold loneliness when the world outside seemed an extension of it.

Frustration welled within her and expanded until she thought she would burst. She was sick of missing Dan, sick of the pressure of the deadline, sick of the project itself. How could such an exciting venture have deteriorated into such a dreadful chore? Tonight she would take a break from it. She would talk the office gang into going to Josie's for the Friday night sing-along and barbeque. But no, that wasn't possible, Deborah remembered with a heavier sigh. Fred and Josie, unable to abide the noise and disruption of demolition, had gone to Florida until construction on the project was well underway. Enterprising Josie had arranged to swap houses with a Florida couple who wanted to spend the winter months skiing.

Disconsolately, she sat down at the curved cherry desk,

propped her elbows on it, and with her chin resting on the heel of her hand, recalled life before Dan. What halcyon days they had been! If they were dull, she hadn't noticed—or minded. They had been peaceful, that was the important thing. There had been no headaches, no tears in the night. She had been satisfied to have her work, Randall and Bea, the house in the foothills, and Dempsey. The security of a pleasant social life, generous income, and growing professional reputation had provided all the excitement she thought she needed.

Her heart was not ready for Dan Parker. She had not been free of pain long enough to endure the kind of grief that loving him could mean.

She had closed her eyes in thought and did not see or hear the door to the office open or the approach of footsteps. "What you need," said the richly toned voice coming from the other side of the desk, "is a weekend away from the drawing board."

Deborah blinked and lifted her chin. "If I'm dreaming, don't tell me," she said rising, unable to accept the vision of Dan in an overcoat and carrying a briefcase as more than a miracle of wishful thinking.

Smiling, he set the briefcase purposefully on the desk and walked around it, his distinctive hair and eyes and brows in striking contrast to the deeply bronzed skin, a result of the desert sun. "Maybe this will prove that you're not," Dan said, bringing his head down, possessing her mouth with such intimacy that she gasped, opening her lips to his passion. Her arms went around him, and she returned his kiss with a fierce hunger, all restraint gone, only her need of him important. After a few moments, Dan said, "Push the intercom button and tell Bea you're going home."

"Well, stop that so I can," she said thickly.

It was only four o'clock, but darkness had almost descended

by the time they reached Deborah's house. Dan had followed her in a four-wheel-drive Bronco outfitted with a telephone, which he had driven from Phoenix. He parked it in the garage on the other side of Deborah's car and, taking her keys, went through the house to the back door to let Dempsey in from the backyard while she picked up her mail.

The dog greeted him ecstatically, dragging his doggy towel to Dan for him to wipe his snowy paws. Dan laughed and bent to the task. "You're quite a mutt, Demps!" he said, thinking how good it was to be here. He had gauged correctly that it was time to put in another appearance. Deborah's happiness at seeing him left little doubt that she was in love with him. He hoped so. He very much wanted Deborah Standridge to fall in love with him. He noted the bars on the windows with a mixture of relief and distaste.

"Shall I make us some coffee?" Deborah asked, coming into the kitchen. "What can I get you?"

"You," he said, going to her and slipping his arms around her waist. "Just you."

"Well," she said shamelessly, throwing all caution, all the careful Savannah breeding to the wind, "we'll have to go upstairs for that."

She loved him. She loved him totally and eternally. There was no turning the truth aside. It flowed into her heart like an inexorable tide, overturning all barriers. The knowledge should have filled her with a wondrous happiness, but it did not. She hadn't the slightest idea of her importance to him in the scheme of his life, his work. She had no idea of how to tell him about Roger. She knew only that she had embarked on a journey from which there was no returning. She must see it through to the end, no matter where it might lead.

Dan stirred, feeling her gaze. "Hello," he said, his eyes still closed. "What are you thinking?"

That I love you, her heart answered. "How would you like to go downstairs with me for some eggs and toast and then a long walk in the snow?"

Dan chuckled. "Sounds like a good idea. What time is it?"

"Two A.M. The snow has stopped."

Deborah prepared them omelets, toast, and cocoa. After eating, they dressed warmly, roused Dempsey, and still warmed by the cocoa, stepped out into a white world. Their breath wreathed out before them in the clear, sharp air. Only the crunch of their footsteps over snow and the occasional murmur of their voices disturbed the brittle night silence. Hand in hand, shoulder brushing shoulder, they tramped through a glistening infinity of snow and stars and close, black sky. For Deborah it was a memorable half hour. If nothing remained at the end, there would still be this memory, set in time, of the two of them alone on such a night.

At breakfast they planned their weekend. Both were eager to try the slopes. Dan had brought his skis from Phoenix, so Deborah suggested they drive to Vail on Sunday and return by nightfall. Dempsey would have to remain behind. His doghouse was warm and spacious, and he was needed "to guard the drawings," Deborah said to Dan with a wry grin. Now when she left the house, even to go for an hour's grocery shopping, she always locked the documents in the safe. Dan gently tapped her chin. "Better safe than sorry," he countered.

They agreed that Saturday had to be a workday for both of them, but in the evening they would go out to dinner. She whistled when he named the restaurant, knowing it to be the poshest in Denver. "And I have a surprise for you," he said.

They had just sat down to their work, Deborah in her

119

workroom and Dan at the kitchen table with a briefcase of papers, when Dempsey set up a ruckus in the backyard. She joined Dan at the glass door and ordered, "Dempsey, stop that!" when she saw him nudging something gray on the snow. When the Labrador persisted, Deborah hurried out into the morning air, sharp as broken glass, to investigate. It moved, and Deborah saw that it was a large gray bird struggling to get away from the dog. She had run out without her jacket, and Dan stayed behind to get it. By the time he joined her, she was hunched over the bird protectively. Dan threw the jacket around her shoulders and grabbed Dempsey by the collar.

"It's a falcon," she said, "a peregrine falcon. There's a nest of them up there in the mountain. This one has been shot."

Holding Dempsey back, Dan noticed a spill of blood, startlingly red, leaching into the snow. The creature's large-pupiled gaze was intent upon Deborah's face as she held it. "Watch out for that beak, honey," Dan warned, worried that the bird might be a carrier of disease. But even as he spoke, the bird's thin lids slowly lowered, and the short, curved beak unhinged. After a final, pitiable twitch, the bird lay still. "Honey—" Dan touched her shoulder. "Take Dempsey inside, and I'll bury it outside the fence."

But Deborah did not move. She continued to stare at the bird, her hair ruffled by a sudden light wind springing from nowhere, like a spirit passing, Dan thought.

"There's a shovel in the garage," she said at last. "I thank you, Dan. Dempsey, come with me."

Back in the kitchen, Deborah decided to make a fresh pot of coffee to steady her shaking hands before taking them back to the drawing board. She mustn't let what had just happened spoil the few precious hours of the weekend. Dan was returning to Phoenix Monday morning. But the fact was, the falcon had reminded her of Estelle Lawson. That accusing stare, as if she were somehow responsible for its death, had been so like the one that had troubled her dreams for years. Like the falcon, the woman had probably died with accusation still in her eyes, un-forgiving to the end.

At the back door, Dan stamped snow from his shoes, watching her through the glass. She kept her back to him when he came into the kitchen. "That was a shame," he said. "Some deer hunter probably bagged the poor bugger. I buried it deep enough to keep from marauders."

"That was good of you," Deborah said, turning to hand him a steaming cup of coffee. She kissed his cold lips lightly, pressing her cheek against his for a moment. "I think I'll go back to work now. See you at lunch."

"Deborah?" He searched her face with a frown. "Don't go back to work yet. You're still disturbed by the death of that bird, aren't you? Sit down and have a cup of coffee with me. You'll feel better."

"I always feel better about everything when I'm with you." She smiled, appreciating the kind of man he was. Taking her cup to the table, she drew out a chair. "You may think this is silly, but that falcon, the accusing way it looked at me, made me think of a woman I once hurt very badly. I was engaged to her son. He had two older sisters, and they meant very much to Estelle, but the sun rose and set on Roger." Deborah took a sip of coffee to moisten her throat, aware that Dan was watching and listening intently.

"What happened?" he asked quietly.

"I broke our engagement almost on the eve of our wedding—"

It was not possible to continue. There was something about Dan's listening attitude, the tension of his posture, that made the words stick in her throat. Was he bothered by the knowledge that she had once been engaged to another man?

"Anyway," she said on a conclusive note, "his mother never forgave me. I can't say that I blame her."

"Did you love…Roger?"

Deborah's gaze was direct. "No. That is why I didn't marry him." Decisively, she pushed back her chair and rose. "It's still a painful subject and one that I can't bring myself to discuss. I don't know why I brought it up."

"Were your parents understanding about the broken engagement?" Dan seemed determined to press the subject.

"I should say not. They were deeply shocked and hurt. They never forgave me for the shame I brought to the family name. Family names are very important in Savannah." She smiled fleetingly, desperate to leave the kitchen before Dan could ask her anything more about Roger. "I really have to get back to work, Dan."

"Is that all of the story?" he persisted, his gaze deeply penetrating.

"It is for now," she said firmly.

In the studio she sat down and pressed a fist to her forehead in despair. Why in the world had she brought the subject up? What an insane, stupid thing to do! Now Dan would be curious and would want to know more about the man she had almost married. It was only natural. He wouldn't now. But in some unguarded, intimate moment, he could very well ask: "What happened to Roger, honey? Where is he now?"

At lunch Dan knocked on the studio door. "Soup's on," he called, "literally." When she opened it, Deborah could smell the aroma of tomato soup heating. The breakfast bar was set with placemats, napkins, and spoons. "I took the liberty of rummaging," Dan said, ladling soup into bowls. "I hope this suits your fancy." He had found crackers, too, and cheese and apples.

Deborah sat down at the bar and sniffed approvingly. "You are an enterprising man, dear sir, very handy to have around."

"I'm glad you think so," he said.

Her stomach was in knots, but she ate the soup and skillfully guided the conversation away from any subject that might lead back to their previous discussion. "What's my surprise?" she asked.

Dan shook his head. "Uh-uh, not until tonight."

After lunch he followed her into the studio. "What are you working on now?" he asked, studying the aerial perspective of the Parker complex tacked on the wall. His headquarters structure rose majestically from the midst of the surrounding buildings, adding grace to the Denver skyline. His eyes shone as he studied it.

"The portico of the bank building," she answered, amused and pleased at his expression. "The drawings of the support columns were finished and given to John, our structural engineer, with little loss from the schedule I'm happy to say."

Around the room she had tacked the aerial perspectives of all her building designs. She watched as Dan inspected each once. "Remarkable," he breathed in admiration. "For just a kid in the business, you've done a lot, haven't you? But I have to say," he said, standing once more before the view of the seven-story gem of corporate beauty and function, "that the Cutter Street complex will be your crowning design."

"Well, we'll see," Deborah said. She would not have shared her misgivings with anyone, but sometimes in the anxiety of meeting the deadline, she felt apprehensive about the complex. The theft of the drawings had seemed like a bad omen. She was uneasy that the plans would not be subjected to the usual thorough examination for errors before being released to the city planning and zoning office.

In the late afternoon, Dan jogged off down the road for his daily five-mile run while she took Dempsey for a walk to shake off the confinement of the house. The earlier disquiet had fled, willed away by the determination to let nothing interfere with the weekend with Dan. Deborah was looking forward to the evening, eager to learn the nature of the surprise Dan had promised.

At the foot of the stairs when he returned, Deborah suggested, "Meet you in the living room at six-thirty? Then will you tell me about my surprise?" His face glowing red from the cold and exertion, Dan consulted the strange looking black-banded jogger's watch he wore.

"You will know at exactly seven o'clock," he said. "We should have time for a drink before it arrives."

"Oh, you!" She swatted his shoulder in frustration. "You're such a tease!"

Deborah had already planned what she would wear, worried only that the silk evening shoes that matched her dress would be ruined by the snow. Although the evening ahead would be exciting and a welcome change from so many evenings alone lately, it would still have been cozy to stay in tonight and enjoy the comfort of the fire. More snow was expected, and it was such a cold, wet night for driving. The traffic and road conditions would demand the attention they could be giving each other.

She heard stereo music as she came down the stairs, indicating that Dan had preceded her to the living room. She paused in the doorway to observe him, a man of such masculine splendor that she wondered how she could ever have thought him attainable. He was at the barred picture window, gazing out at the night. Lamplight gleamed on the well-groomed hair and the faultless tailoring of the dark blue suit. He turned at her entrance.

"Good Lord, Deborah," he exclaimed softly, his whole being expressing stunned admiration.

Deborah relaxed and said with a laugh, "You look heartbreakingly handsome yourself."

Dan approached, drinking her in with his eyes. "Heartbreaking?"

"That's an old Southern expression. It's used to describe the kind of boy a girl can never hope to capture just for herself but can enjoy only for a little while, like a perfect day that you can't hold forever."

"Is that what you think I am, a passing day that you can't hold forever?"

She had led them to a precipice, she realized, dropping her eyes to the knot of his striped silk tie. She couldn't answer that question, not yet. Neither could he. He knew so little about her. He did not know about Roger. "It's too soon for questions like that," she answered gently, her throat tightening. She could not imagine her tomorrows without Dan. "A day at a time leads to forever—maybe," she added, looking at him.

Disappointment lay a moment in his eyes. Then he bent and lightly kissed the side of her mouth. "I must make a point to make each one special," he said, letting the moment pass. "And speaking of special, I believe I hear your surprise. It's here early."

"*Hear* my surprise?"

"Where is your coat?"

"Why, in the hall." She had hung it there when she came downstairs, a pearl gray silver fox to complement her silver lamé dinner dress. As Dan helped her into it, the door chimes sounded. Dan's height and size obstructed the caller from view, but in the drive she could see part of a long, shining, black hood.

"Dan!" she burst out, rushing to peer round his shoulder. A chauffeur in livery stood at the door, and in the circular drive was a long, sleek limousine. The driver touched his black-billed cap when he saw Deborah, rendered momentarily speechless by her beauty. "I don't believe it," she cried. "I just don't believe it! I was so worried about going out on a night like tonight, not being able to talk to you because you'd be concentrating on driving. Now, we get to enjoy every minute! Oh, Dan, how thoughtful of you!" she cried in pleasure, peering into the sumptuous interior.

"I think you've made a hit, sir," said the chauffeur, grinning.

"It would seem so." Dan chuckled, delighted at her pleasure. "I'd say it's the only conveyance worthy of her tonight, wouldn't you?" Both were smiling at her.

"Indeed I do, sir."

The driver bowed her into the spacious backseat while Dan locked the front door. There was Champagne, of course, cooling in ice in a deep well of the ingeniously constructed bar. The napkin had slipped, and Deborah saw that it was a vintage Dom Perignon. Dan pushed a button when he joined her, and as the limousine pulled out of the drive, a glass partition noiselessly glided up between them and the driver. They grinned at each other and met halfway for a kiss. "You're such a nice man," she said.

"I hope you will always think so," he answered. His eyes ran over her in a caress. How beautifully that fur set off the luster of her hair, the purity of her skin. Her eyes shone with a happiness he had never seen before. Good. He must get her to trust him, to believe him. "Just a prelude," he said, "for what I hope will be a memorable evening." He poured them each a chilled glass of the costly vintage, opened by the driver the moment he'd arrived. They touched glasses. "To us, Deborah—to whatever that may mean."

"I'll drink to that," she said, blushing slightly under the directness of the blue gaze.

"I think you should be a tour director for the Tourist Bureau of Colorado in your spare time," Dan drawled as they trudged with their shoulder-supported skis down the narrow streets of Vail toward the chairlifts that would take them to the slopes known as the Back Bowls, recommended for expert skiers only. Deborah had just finished acquainting Dan with some of the history of the village, patterned after several of the skiing meccas of Europe. Deborah appreciated its Alpine architecture and the fact that no cars were allowed on the streets. They had to be left in the parking areas outside the town.

"Maybe I will if I ever lose my job." She laughed. "It may make a nice change."

"You getting tired of your job?" Dan asked in surprise.

"Only of deadlines," she said, wrinkling her nose at him.

Dan was a strong skier, but Deborah's skill was a match for his strength. In perfect alignment, at one with snow and wind and speed, they schussed together down the uninterrupted expanses of treeless terrain, the snow-like powder beneath their skis. At the completion of one run, Dan grinned at her, his eyes as brilliantly blue as the sky behind his head. "Looks as if we've found something else we do well together."

At the end of the final run, the sun began to set, and in silence they watched as the snow-clad mountain turned a molten red in the wash of its brilliant rays. In awe, their hands met and held tightly. "I think we've just been given some kind of blessing," Dan said.

That night as they lay together in blissful fatigue from the day, Deborah said, "Thank you for coming this weekend. I needed the pleasure of your company."

Dan propped up on an elbow to observe her. "I won't be able to get back, Deborah, until I return to take the plans to the zoning office. That's about three weeks away. Will they be ready?"

"Yes, Mr. Parker. I promised they would."

"Don't be brusque and businesslike."

"You're the one who brought up business."

Dan sighed and fiddled with the lace cuff of her sleeve. "So I did. Forgive me. It's just that...this complex means so much to me, honey. It's the culmination of all my dreams, all my work."

"Dan, the plans will be ready on schedule. I'm surprised that you're not more worried about the zoning commission approving them on time. What if they should *not* approve them for some reason?"

"Well, now, my dear, that's what I'm paying the Hayden firm a hefty commission to avoid."

"Oh, damn!" Deborah bounced out of bed, accidentally striking Dempsey on the rump. They'd allowed him to remain for the night since he'd spent the day in the backyard. He let out a startled yelp. "Sorry, Demps. Go back to sleep," she said and reached for her robe.

"Where are you going?"

"Downstairs for some milk—to drown my disappointment."

"Disappointment?" Dan sounded bewildered.

"Yes! Randall warned me that corporate business came first with you."

"Oh, he did, did he?" Dan followed her down the stairs, flapping into his robe. "Maybe you'd better explain that."

"Well, first," she whirled to him, "let me explain this. After the most perfect weekend of my life, after I've been whisked

off in a limousine to the most expensive restaurant in town, followed by a glorious night of love, followed by the finest skiing
day in my experience, you lie in my bed the last night you're
here and have the audacity to bring up business!"

"That was obviously not a bright move on my part."

"You're so right; it wasn't."

"Now let's get back to Randall. Just exactly what has he been
saying to you about me?"

"Nothing I wouldn't have picked up in the articles I read
about you when I was designing your headquarters."

"Which is?"

"That business, making money, is your whole life. Oh, you're
considered a nice guy, noted for your building integrity and all
that. But your wife, your lover, your mistress, your—everything
is business. You give it your primary allegiance, love, and time,
and there's no room in your life for anything else. That's what
Randall warned me about."

Dan allowed an expletive to express his thoughts on Randall's opinion of him. Then he demanded, "I want to know
what *you* think."

"I don't know," Deborah said. "I honestly don't. Just when I
think I'm making a space in your life, something comes up related to business that makes me feel tossed out on my ear."

"You're referring to the theft of the documents, aren't you,
and how I jumped all over you?"

"As I recall, that happened after another perfect day."

"Honey—" Dan went to her, and she let him take her into his
arms. "I admit that business has been the sum of my existence.
It still is, maybe. I don't know. All I know for sure is that I used
to work all day to the exclusion of anyone or anything else in my
thoughts, but not anymore. I think about you constantly. I miss
you. I want to be with you. You *are* making a space in my life.

A big one. Please believe that. I'm just happy you want to be in it. You've never told me that before."

"Did I have to?" she murmured, her anger all gone.

"Forget the milk," Dan said huskily. "Let's go back upstairs."

The next morning while Dan cleared away their breakfast dishes, Deborah telephoned the Hayden firm to inform Bea that she would be late for the usual Monday staff meeting. She was chagrined that, as luck would have it, Randall answered. After he mentioned that Bea would be out for the morning because of a dentist's appointment, Deborah explained her purpose for calling. "I've a friend who needs a ride to the airport," she began, but Randall cut her off.

"Deborah, I am aware that Dan Parker was in the office Friday, so you may refer to him by name," he said frostily. "Surely, he can make his own arrangements for getting to the airport."

"He could, I suppose, Randall, but I prefer to drive him."

"You left early Friday because of Dan. Doesn't he realize you have work to do? After all, it's *his* project!"

"Randall, for goodness sake!" Deborah was calling from the hall phone, and just at that moment, Dan passed through on his way to the guest room. He stopped short at her exclamation. Calmly she said, "Please inform the staff that I have finished the drawings of the bank portico and will begin the restaurant today. I'll be there just as soon as I can."

"You know, of course, dear child, that you completely forgot about my bridge party yesterday. I say *forgot* because I know you would have had the courtesy to inform me that you would not be coming had you remembered to do so. It was a most trying experience, not to say an embarrassing one, to try to find a fourth when you didn't show up."

Deborah was shocked at her oversight. She had never once thought of Randall's third-Sunday-of-the-month bridge party after Dan opened the door to her office. "I am so sorry, Randall. It was dreadfully rude of me, but I truly did forget."

"Obviously. We'll discuss it later. Please try to make it to work as soon as possible." Without a further word, he hung up.

"What's the matter, honey?" Dan asked as she slowly replaced the receiver. He came up behind her with a frown. "Is Randall giving you a hard time about something?"

"His bridge party yesterday. It completely slipped my mind, and he's in one of his quiet rages about it. I can't say that I blame him."

"Look, if it's going to present a problem for you at the office, I can get a cab to the airport."

"No, the damage is already done." She gave him a quick smile. "I might as well be hanged for a sheep as a lamb."

But the traffic was so snarled due to snow that when they reached the airport, there was no time for a last cup of coffee together. Dan gave his luggage to the porter, then came around to open her door. Deborah scooted over a little to allow room for the silver-gray head, for the privacy of their last precious moment together. "Good-bye for a while," she whispered. It was all her closed throat would permit her to say.

"Until the twenty-second," he said and pressed a hard kiss upon her lips.

It was sleeting by the time she pulled into her parking space at the office. She let herself in the side door, dabbed at her eyes, checked her lipstick. Then she walked down to the conference room and quietly slipped into her seat. Randall was holding forth. He ignored her entrance, but from the look John Turner sent her way, she knew that in her absence she had been reprimanded.

By four o'clock, sleet had completely encrusted the bay window. Deborah was at the drawing board, her spirits as overcast as the sky outside when the intercom buzzed. It was Bea. "Come see what's arrived for you, Deborah."

With an eager smile, the secretary waited for Deborah to remove the florist's paper from a tall arrangement of flowers. They were roses, two dozen long-stemmed tight red buds sprigged with fern and delicate baby's breath. Slowly, holding her breath, Deborah removed not the usual florist's card from the envelope, but a memo slip embossed with the name of Dan's company. She knew that Dan had ordered the flowers in the last few minutes before he boarded his plane. On the slip was drawn a circle. Above it was written: "This circle represents my life. The black areas represent the space you fill in it." Tears blurred her eyes. The entire circle had been shaded black.

Chapter Nine

The construction documents were finished! They had been placed in the center of the conference table to be relished as a job well done. Randall beamed at his staff assembled for its Monday morning meeting. "If I had my *druthers*," he twinkled at the digression from his usual vocabulary, "it would be, of course, that the documents could have been finished early enough to run them through a quality-control check. However, completing them on time has been miraculous enough, and I extend to you all my warmest congratulations."

His smile lessened noticeably as he addressed Deborah. "When will Mr. Parker be arriving for them? He has not seen fit to take me into his confidence. No doubt he has you."

Everyone, even John Turner, avoided looking at Deborah. It had become obvious that Deborah had fallen from grace. Rumor had it that Randall disapproved of her "romantic involvement," as Bea phrased it, with the builder of the project. In staff meetings of the past three weeks, he had missed no opportunity to allude to the affair and remind her that he was displeased. Deborah had met his disdain with quiet dignity.

Now she answered steadily, "His plane will be arriving this afternoon. He'll come by the office to pick them up so that he can have them at the city planning office first thing in the morning."

"Why come here? You'll certainly be seeing him this evening. Why can't you simply take the documents with you after work?"

"I do not want the responsibility of having them in my possession," she answered levelly.

"Very wise," Randall said with a tepid smile. "Especially in the light of the theft you recently experienced. Tell Mr. Parker he will find the documents in my office."

That afternoon Deborah did not attend the celebration party in the production room. Not even the anticipation of seeing Dan within the hour could ease her pain. She was suffering from the knowledge that a rare and irreplaceable affection was crumbling, and she was powerless to prevent it.

The last confrontation with Randall over Dan had been bitter. It had happened the morning of Dan's departure for Phoenix. She had been summoned to Randall's office and there, with a look of utter disgust distorting his sensitive features, Randall had termed her intimacy with Dan "a sordid little affair." Since then he had hardly spoken to her. She looked up from her desk in surprise, therefore, when Randall came into the office carrying two glasses of Champagne.

"A peace offering," he said, "with the hope that you will forgive me."

Deborah took the proffered glass. "If it was your intention to hurt me, Randall, you've succeeded," she said quietly.

Randall sighed disconsolately and strolled to the bay window. "I know," he said, looking out at the snow-covered landscape. "I've not been proud of myself lately. I've seen a side of me that I never knew existed until three weeks ago when you told me that you were in love with Dan Parker. The knowledge, the pain of it, has brought out the worst in me. I can only hope you will understand that I've been acting out of the anguish of my disappointment."

Deborah looked at him sorrowfully. "Disappointment, Randall? But why are you so disappointed? Is it solely because Dan Parker is the man I love and not someone else you consider more suitable?"

"No, child." Randall turned to look at her, and Deborah saw the disturbance in the gentle blue eyes. "I guess that I never expected you to…" he hesitated over his choice of words, "fall in love. There have been so many eligible, worthy men in your life, but you were impervious to them all. You seemed…above the desires of the flesh, the needs of ordinary women. You cared only for your work, the firm, for Bea and me. Frankly, I had become used to the idea that you would always belong solely to us, take over the firm when I retired, inherit it upon my death." He gave a heavy sigh and shook his head. "That you have met someone in the space of two short months to whom you've obviously given so much," he went on, "and from whom you hope for marriage and children, has been rather a shock to me."

Deborah got up from the desk, tears shimmering in her eyes, and drew him close. "But, Randall, you could be a part of it all. Why, you'd make a wonderful grandfather," she said exuberantly. "Do you think I wouldn't want you and Bea to share in my life still, that I wouldn't need you anymore?"

"And what about your talent, my dear? What would become of that between diaper changes and housekeeping chores?"

"Is my talent so important when compared to the love of a husband and family, the making of a home?" It was a new and startling consideration. Deborah realized in amazement that if Dan married her, she would gladly set aside her career for a while, as long as it took to raise children in a loving, nurturing atmosphere. The idea thrilled her. To have a happy home and family of her own—now *that* would be a crowning design!

"You would sacrifice your career for the nebulous rewards of child rearing and husband pampering?" Randall was shocked.

"Many women are able to manage both," she pointed out, trying to get him to envision gains rather than losses.

But Randall shook his head. "No, my dear. A talent like yours, in order to realize its fullest potential, must be kept pure from mundane concerns."

"Randall, I can't believe you feel that way!"

He patted her hand. "Alas, but I do, my child. But let us return to the subject of Dan. I still very much fear for you in your relationship with him. However, if you must love him, you must. There is no accounting for the indiscriminate visitation of that emotion upon two people. I will try to accept your feelings for him as graciously as possible. And I trust you will find it in your heart to forgive my conduct of the last three weeks."

"You know I do. I just wish you could be happy for me."

"I will when I've been given sufficient reason. As of our last discussion, Dan had not, ah, avowed his feelings for you. Has that status changed?"

"No," Deborah replied, "but he's invited me to return with him to Phoenix for Thanksgiving. That's a good sign, don't you think?"

"Well," Randall considered, "in my day it was. Such an invitation was usually tendered to the young lady for the reason of meeting the man's parents. Er, uh, whom are you going to meet?"

"Hang on to your socks, dear," Deborah warned with a grin. "Alicia Dameron."

Randall's eyes widened. "Alicia Dameron! Dan's old flame? Oh, dear—" His delicate brow crimped into a series of fine wrinkles. "I *am* out of step with the times!"

Deborah laughed and squeezed his arm affectionately. "It

does seem unusual, doesn't it? I suppose I should be jealous, but I'm not. I don't know exactly how to feel about seeing her, but I do genuinely believe that whatever was between them in the past is over now. They're just very good friends, like family it seems, and Dan says that Alicia is dying to meet me. This four-day weekend coming up is a perfect opportunity. Dan and I will fly to Phoenix together, then drive back. This time he'll be staying in Denver until the plans are approved."

"I am sure you'll like that." Randall's smile was fragile. Again he shook his head. "It's a different world, to be sure, than when I was a young man, but I wish you a splendid trip. Bea and I will miss you, of course. We've not missed many Thanksgivings together, have we? What arrangements have you made for Dempsey while you are gone?"

"He'll have to go to a kennel, I'm afraid."

"Oh, but he can't!" Randall protested. "Dempsey is too big for a kennel. What if I come out and housesit for you? Your house shouldn't be left unattended anyway. Thievery is rampant during the holidays. Bea can come, too, and we can go on some short hiking expeditions into the foothills. We haven't done that for a long time."

"Randall, Dempsey will love you forever!" cried Deborah gratefully. The world was suddenly becoming all sunshine and warmth. "I hadn't wanted to leave him in a kennel. He would feel so abandoned."

"We must spare him that feeling, mustn't we?" Randall's lips twisted with faint irony. "It's the worst feeling in the world. Don't forget to leave me a set of keys."

When he had gone, Deborah raised the glass of Champagne to her lips in a thoughtful glow. Randall had not been able to resist that parting shot, but she felt no rancor toward him now. He did feel abandoned. She understood his feelings and felt very sorry for him, a childless, aging widower whose only involvement with a woman had been the clearly platonic one he had shared with Bea all these years. Deborah could not imagine that he had ever known passion, the extreme compelling urgency eating through one like fire, to fuse in a single union with another human being.

Deborah took her reflections and the glass of Champagne to the bay window and the aspen tree. What an ironic surprise that she wanted, after all, the life that her parents had tried to impose upon her.

A pair of large hands closed round her shoulders. "Hello, my beauty," said Dan, his voice husky and close, his breath warm as he pressed a kiss on her neck. The presence of him was enfolding, igniting. She relaxed against him, savoring the feel of him, anticipating the moment she would turn.

In the night Deborah awoke, suddenly and completely. Dan lay asleep beside her, stretched out full length. She raised up to peer down at Dempsey curled in sound slumber on his pallet. The stars were overcast tonight. All was quiet, deep, dark. Yet she had been awakened by the revisitation of something—a dream, a memory, an idea—having, of all things, to do with Dempsey. It was like a feeling of déjà vu. Only recently—she couldn't remember when—she had felt the same nameless exhortation, like an urgent voice lost on the wind trying to impart a crucial message that she must understand before it was too late.

Deborah lay back down and breathed deeply to calm the palpitations of her heart. How ridiculous that a night that followed such a gratifying series of events should be interrupted by a nightmare. She glanced over at Dan, sleeping soundly. Well he might. The construction documents had been completed on time. They were ready for the final phase of verification before their execution into reality. She was positive the zoning commission would find no fault with the plans. They met every safety requirement, considered every public need from bathroom facilities to parking spaces for the handicapped. By the middle of December, the documents would be returned with the commission's full approval to begin construction. Dan's dream would be under way to fulfillment.

Then why this palpitating heart? she wondered. *Why the pinprick of concern in the back of my mind?* She didn't want to become like her mother, who used to worry over nothing.

"Go easy on that," Dan admonished as Deborah took a sip of the Champagne just served the first-class passengers. "You haven't had anything to eat today, I'd bet."

They were airborne, leaving the glistening white peaks of the Colorado Rockies for the vast brown stretches of the Arizona desert. Temperatures were in the seventies there, Dan had said, just right for swimming. Deborah hoped so. After the pressure of the last nine weeks, she could think of no better way to recharge the batteries than to lie around a swimming pool, soaking up the sun.

"I've been too excited to eat today," Deborah said, relishing the Champagne, snuggling down into the comfort of the first-class seat. "This tastes wonderful. Now tell me again what we're going to do in Phoenix?"

Dan made a great show of turning his head in surprise, the hike of his brows clearly asking, *all* that we're going to do?

"No, silly." She giggled, the Champagne already at work in her bloodstream.

"Tonight when we arrive, we're going to my condominium. You'll meet my housekeeper, Mrs. Watson. She's been with me for years and will move to Denver once I've built a house there—"

"You plan to build a house in Denver?" Deborah interrupted, letting the stewardess refill her glass.

"That's my plan. Do you think you might like to design it? I won't be getting around to it for a while, not until the headquarters are finished and the company is transferred to Denver. But yes, eventually, I'd like to have a home of my own in Denver. I'm getting tired of town houses and condominiums."

"They say that happens to bachelors." Deborah's eyes widened ingenuously. "You were saying about Mrs. Watson?"

Dan's expression did not change by a flicker of an eyelash. He went on blandly, "She'll have a grand meal prepared, I'm sure. She's a great cook. You'll like her."

"What will Mrs. Watson think about…you and me…about my staying with you?"

"Mrs. Watson is not one to question or comment. She was told to prepare the guest bedroom. Whatever conclusions she draws she will keep to herself."

"I would imagine," Deborah could not resist commenting, "that your Mrs. Watson has had numerous occasions on which to draw conclusions."

Dan smiled across at her and fondled her hand. "Jealous?"

"Yes," she admitted frankly.

"Good. That's a telling sign."

"Of what?"

"That you're falling under my spell."

Whatever that means, thought Deborah. *Why can't he tell me he loves me?* "So continue with the schedule of events," she urged.

Dan explained that they would be going to Alicia's for Thanksgiving dinner. There would be two other guests, both men, Alicia's agent and attorney. "She'll probably cook the meal herself. In your honor she's preparing cornbread stuffing for the turkey. Do you like cornbread stuffing?"

"Very much. It's called *dressing*, though. Cornbread dressing. That's awfully nice of her, Dan. Imagine—having Thanksgiving dinner cooked by a movie star! You know," she turned to him matter-of-factly, "you've brought a number of surprises into my life."

Dan lifted her fingertips to his lips, his gaze engaging hers. "I hope to bring you many more," he said softly.

Mrs. Watson opened the door to them with a broad smile. She was an angular woman whose gray hair and numerous wrinkles suggested an age in the late fifties. Dan had said the woman was a widow whose only child had been killed in Vietnam. "Welcome to Phoenix, Miss Standridge, to Mr. Parker's home. I have heard nothing but good things about you."

Her friendliness eased Deborah's embarrassment immediately and indicated that perhaps the woman had drawn some conclusions after all, and favorable ones, too. It was an uplifting thought.

At the swimming pool the next morning, Deborah drew the eyes of all those who had come out on their patios with newspapers and coffee cups. Dan had already whistled his approval of the bathing suit. "But I am so white!" she despaired, looking down at her pale limbs.

"What can you expect of a Colorado snow bunny? You're lucky to have the kind of skin that doesn't burn. By the time we leave, you'll have a tan."

She already had a smattering of one, Deborah discovered, as she dressed for Alicia's Thanksgiving dinner party. Her skin radiated a healthy glow, a flattering foil for the ivory Grecian dress so suited to the line of her figure. She had brought along a rope of pearls with a turquoise and diamond clasp to set off the dress. There was a matching bracelet, legacies from her mother.

A number of times during the drive to Alicia's house in Scottsdale, a suburb of Phoenix, Deborah felt Dan's eyes leave the road and wander over to her. She sat in a delicious glow of excitement, her eyes presumably on the famous Camelback Mountain looming in the distance. It seemed to her like an extension upward of the desert itself since no trees and little vegetation grew on it. But her mind, her heart, her body throbbed with awareness of the man beside her and the pleasurable certainty that he loved her. It was only a matter of time, perhaps during this weekend, that he would declare it.

Alicia herself opened the door to her rambling, white-stuccoed, Spanish-inspired mansion. "Deborah," she fluted, extending a diamond-beringed hand, long red fingernails glistening. "I knew you would be exquisite. Welcome."

"Thank you," said Deborah, enveloped at once in the breathtaking essence of all that was Alicia Dameron. Dan seemed totally inured.

"Hello, princess," he greeted her, casually kissing the proffered cheek. "I'm hungry as a bear. When do we eat?"

"Shortly. Deborah, how do you stand him?"

"Easy." Deborah smiled.

"Good for you," said the actress.

After dinner, their hostess left the men with cigars and brandy on the deck of the sparkling blue swimming pool to take Deborah on a tour of the house. Once alone, Alicia minced no words. "Has he told you yet that he loves you?"

Deborah was too amused by Alicia's directness to be taken aback. For all her dazzling beauty, fame, and diamonds, the actress was what people from the South termed "down-home folks."

142

"No, he hasn't," she answered.

"Have you told him how you feel?"

"No," said Deborah.

With a lavish flash of the diamond rings, Alicia demanded, "Well, why ever not? It's plain as mud on a clean floor that you two are mad about each other. What are you waiting for?"

"I've not wanted to rush things. Dan is the kind of man who has to have time to live with new feelings. I must be a new feeling for him; I might even be a threat to his concentration on business. Except for you, he has never permitted a woman to take precedence over it."

"Oh, that—" Alicia airily waved aside that notion. "I never took precedence over anything in Dan's life, not in the way you mean. I happened to come along when his life was at a low ebb. He was hurting from the loss of a childhood friend in a car accident, a man he loved like a brother. You probably know that Dan's mother died when he was very young. Even though his father was still living until a few years ago, Dan was practically an orphan. He adored the mother of the fellow who was killed. I guess she had sort of taken him under her wing and treated him like another son. She was a strong influence in his life, probably the main reason he's a wealthy man today. Anyway, when her son was killed, she sort of shriveled up like an autumn leaf and died within the year. Dan suffered a double loss—" Alicia broke off at the stark look on Deborah's face. "You didn't know all of this?" Alicia inquired. "Surely Dan told you?"

"No." Deborah shook her head slowly, stunned by the impact of Alicia's revelation. "No, he hasn't."

"Possibly because it's still a very painful subject with him, Deborah. It doesn't mean anything. You have a lifetime to share these things."

For Deborah, the remainder of the visit was torture. She thought it would never end. The chill within her had expanded until she felt it seeping out through her pores, absorbing the warm sun captured earlier in the day. At one point, Dan asked in concern, "Everything okay, honey? You seem awfully quiet."

She managed a convincing smile. "I'm fine. The food and wine have made me drowsy, that's all."

In the evening when they had finally returned to the condominium, Mrs. Watson was just leaving. "I thought I told you to take the day off!" Dan exclaimed. "What are you doing back here?"

"Now don't scold." She wagged a finger at him in affection. "I just came in to tidy up a bit and to make sure everything was in readiness for you young folks to have a nice breakfast in the morning. I don't come in until eleven, you see," she explained to Deborah. "Mr. Parker is one for a nice breakfast, he is. Oh, and Mr. Parker—you know that photograph you always keep on the bureau of your room? It's missing."

"No, it isn't," Dan replied. "I knocked it off accidentally, and the glass broke. I put it away until I can get it replaced."

"Oh," Mrs. Watson said, satisfied, and wished them a good night.

Deborah went out on the patio to wait for Dan to bring her a glass of milk and himself a nightcap. The night air was pleasant and balmy. Lifting her gaze heavenward, she saw that her evening stars followed them to Phoenix. They winked in merry familiarity, insensible to her mood.

Dan came out on the patio and handed her a glass of milk. "Want to tell me about it?" he asked, taking a seat. "Was it anything that Alicia said?"

"Goodness, no," Deborah lied. "She was so friendly and pleasant. I could come to like her very much."

"Then what is it, Deborah?"

Deborah studied the contents of her glass. "Dan…do you think we're going too fast? I mean, we've only known each other a little over two months, and I—I feel that I am getting involved with you more deeply than I—I want to. You're the most exciting man I've ever known. It's been easy to lose my head over you, to forget for a while the—the importance of my career to me."

Dan sat in the shadows. Deborah sensed that he had become motionless. "I thought you wanted some space in my life," he reminded her. His voice had the quiet quality of a rock.

"Well, I did—I do—" She squeezed her eyes shut, as if it hurt to think. "Oh, Dan, I don't know what I'm saying!"

"Then let me interpret, Deborah. You're saying you don't know how you feel about me yet, that I'm rushing you toward something you're not sure you want. Is that what you're trying to tell me?"

Deborah nodded miserably, her eyes downcast. Dan stood up. "I'm sure you can understand if I'm surprised. It seems that I have been sailing in this boat all by myself." Deborah knew he was looking down at her, waiting, hoping for her to speak. She could feel the heavy weight of his disappointment when she did not. "Is there anything else you want to say to me before I say good night?"

"No," she whispered, her head still bent.

"Then you'll find the guest room more than comfortable, I believe. Good night, Deborah."

Dan caught a glimpse of his rigid countenance in the hall mirror as he passed to his room. The desert in the full heat of summer had seldom looked more forbidding. He began undressing, angrily yanking at his tie, chucking cuff links into the jewelry compartment on the top bureau drawer. His eye fell upon a small blue velvet ring box. He took it out and lifted the lid, his mouth tightening. The two-carat solitaire in the Tiffany setting winked back at him playfully, mockingly. He had intended placing the box on Deborah's breakfast plate in the morning. Now he snapped the lid shut and hurled the box back into the bureau drawer before slamming it shut.

In the guest room, Deborah wept bitterly into a pillow long into the night. Lord, she had paid a thousand times for what she had done. Was there never to be a final payment for the tragedy of eight years ago? How cruelly ironic that Dan had been a victim of a tragedy similar to the one she had caused. The loss of his friend, the loss of the woman who had been like a mother to him might just as easily have been Roger and Estelle. Her heart twisted with the memory of Dan's face that one time he had alluded to a low period in his life. Pain, still fresh, had flitted across those clear eyes. He would never be able to forgive her. Her own parents had not. How could Dan?

She had planned to make a clean break of the past this weekend. Now she never would. To tell Dan would mean to risk his rejection, and she could never bear that. There was still the burden of her parents' censure on her shoulders, the weight of Estelle's, the weight of her own. She could not add Dan's.

Chapter Ten

A soft knock came at the door. It was nine o'clock, Deborah was dressed, and her bags were packed. "Yes?" she called.

"How about some of Mrs. Watson's breakfast?" Dan invited through the closed door. "Her feelings will be hurt if we don't at least try it."

Deborah glanced at herself in the mirror. Makeup did not disguise the kind of night she'd had. She took a moment to inhale deeply, to steady her nerves for the ordeal ahead, knowing they were beyond much help. Just his gentle knock, the compassionate timbre of his voice, had brought her to the edge of tears. "Coming," she said.

Dan's eyes dilated in surprise as he took in the traveling suit. He himself was dressed in bathing trunks and a matching shirt, ready for a leisurely morning of swimming and sunbathing. After lunch he planned to take Deborah Christmas shopping along Scottsdale's Fifth Avenue. "What's this?" he asked, glancing at the bags on the bed. "You're not leaving?"

"I'm afraid so, Dan. It was a mistake to come. While you were out jogging, I called the airlines and booked a flight back to Denver. Luckily, I was able to get one—"

"Deborah, you can't leave like this! We can talk out whatever problem you seem to think we have. Running away isn't going to help."

He made a move toward her, but she backed away. "I'm not running away from anything, Dan. I'm going back to something, something I never should have left."

"What the hell are you talking about?"

"My career. For a while I forgot how important it is to me, how all-consuming. I thought I told you last night. Since coming here, I've come to realize that I'm not ready for the direction our relationship seems to be heading. I don't want that kind of commitment yet." Her words sounded thin and hollow; she hardly recognized the sound of her own voice. "If I am flattering myself about your intentions—" she began again, unable to lift her eyes above the region of his Adam's apple, "I—well, chalk it up to the height of female conceit." She shrugged and raised her eyes, smiling weakly. "Or unmitigated gall, brass, nerve, chutzpah, cheek—you name it, I deserve it."

"Cut that out, Deborah!" Dan ordered sharply. Beneath the tan, a flush had swept his face. "I don't care if you miss your plane, we're going to talk about this. You owe me an explanation about this sudden about-face of yours. And quit the cocky wordplay. It's inappropriate at a time like this."

"It isn't an about-face. You just refused to see what you should have seen all along!"

"Enlighten me, please," he drawled.

"My career is my whole life, Dan, just like business is yours. You of all people should understand what my work means to me. I thought it would be fairer to call a—a halt now...than...let us go on." Dan had blurred behind a curtain of tears, and Deborah pushed past the broad shoulders, seeking space, air, water. Her throat felt dry as sand. She plunged toward the kitchen, slowing at the appearance of the brightly set breakfast table. Dear Mrs. Watson! In the center, a yellow ceramic cornucopia brimmed with fresh fruit. Across one plate lay a long-stemmed red rose, and the heavenly smell of baking sweet rolls wafted about the kitchen. Deborah grabbed a glass and turned on the tap. She had to stop crying if this was going to work. Lord! Sometimes it hurt to be alive!

Dan came up behind her as she filled the glass. "This wouldn't have anything to do with taking over as successor to Randall when he retires, would it? Or inheriting the firm when he dies?"

Water sloshed over the sleeve of the suit, saturating the cuff of her silk blouse. Slowly Deborah turned to face him, her mouth and eyes wide in astonishment. "What? How did you know about that?"

Dan eyed her grimly. "Randall told me when I picked up the documents. He made it clear that you would succeed him only if I disappeared from your life. Apparently he thinks you're too good for me or for the marital state, period. I intended to discuss our conversation with you. I didn't want to throw a monkey wrench into your career opportunities, but what I really anticipated hearing was your laugh when I told you about his last-ditch effort to break us up. I know he's tried. I even went so far as wishing I could be a fly on the wall when you stormed into his office Monday morning and told him what he could do with his firm." Dan stepped closer, making no attempt to touch her. The blue eyes flashed with anguish. "Have I really been in this boat all by myself, Deborah?"

He had given her an out, and she had to take it. Tears sprang to her eyes. She shut the lids tightly to prevent their escape. "Yes." She nodded, swallowing. "I just couldn't combine a career and marriage. Neither would be successful." She felt him move away from her, heard the click of the stove as he turned it off. After a long silence, Deborah opened her eyes. He had picked up the rose.

"I had you pegged all wrong, Deborah," he said, meditatively twirling the rose. "I thought you wanted what I did. Marriage, a home, kids. I wouldn't ask you to give up your career, but I would ask you to make a place in it for us. I grew up without a mother, so I have some very specific ideas about the importance of a woman staying home, being home when the kids need her. I expected us to blend our careers. They are a natural for each other. You could pick and choose your hours, even your years."

"And while you were continuing your unimpeded climb to the top of the building industry," she forced bitterness into her tone, "I'd be home wiping noses and cleaning hamster cages."

Dan laid the rose down. A glint of anger appeared in the blue eyes. "Something like that, if the kids needed you to. I realize it's selfish to ask a woman today to do that, but I also realize it's the only way being married to me would work. That's why I've never married." The corners of his lips lifted ironically. "If I seem a man totally dedicated to business, Deborah, it may interest you and Randall to know that I've never had anything else to do with my life until I met you."

Deborah took her eyes away from the tall figure. "I'm so sorry, Dan."

Deborah took a taxi from the airport out to the foothills, her eyes red and swollen, a sodden handkerchief balled in her fist. What a different return to Denver than the one she had envisioned with Dan. The ideal holiday weather was to hold through the weekend, and on Sunday they were to have risen early and driven back in the Mercedes, enjoying each other and the scenery and the music of Dan's tape collection. At noon they planned to stop for a picnic. Now Dan would have a long, lonely drive by himself, with plenty of time to hurt and brood, to think how wrong he had been about the girl he loved. And he did love her, that was the tragedy. He wanted to marry her. He wanted everything she wanted. He had not pegged her wrong. She felt the turn of a new season in her life. She would soon be thirty. Spring was over. It had been a tragic, tumultuous season for her, and she would not be sorry to see it go. Her career and the Hayden firm had been her ballasts during these past stormy years, but that need was over now, thank God. She needed Dan now. She wanted him for all seasons, for every moment of her life. The problem now was whether he would ever want her again.

Rather than let herself in with her keys, Deborah rang the doorbell to alert Bea and Randall of her presence, just in case she was interrupting any sort of romantic goings-on. She thought it unlikely, but one never knew. Her doubt was justified when Randall opened the door. Even at leisure he wore the inevitable bow tie, which today was amusingly incongruous with the rolled-up shirtsleeves, suspenders, her strawberry print apron tied around his middle, and slippers. He carried a spatula and stared at her blankly. "My dear child! We didn't expect you until Sunday!"

"My plans changed." She should be furious with him, but she wasn't. His meddlesome bid to hold on to her, to preserve her from Dan, had provided the escape she needed. "Hello, Dempsey." The big Labrador, wriggling and whining in welcome, had appeared at the sound of her voice. She bent down to hug him, avoiding Randall's curious eyes.

"What in the world happened?" he demanded.

"I came to my senses, that's what happened. I realized that you were right about marriage sapping my creative energies. I'm not ready for that kind of sacrifice yet." She gave the dog a final pat and straightened up. Randall's stricken look was a surprise. She had expected an ear-to-ear grin. "What's the matter? I thought you'd be pleased."

"You're not saying that you and Dan are through?" he asked.

"That's exactly what I'm saying, Randall. It's over between us. Why aren't you happy about it? Isn't this what you wanted?"

"Why, uh, yes, certainly," he said, blinking, coming to himself. "I'm just stunned, that's all. You were so sure of your feelings the last time we spoke. Are you sure about them now?" Eyes narrowed, he considered her closely.

"Yes," Deborah answered sincerely. "I am very sure about my feelings concerning Dan Parker. Let's drop the subject, shall we? Where's Bea?"

"Out on the mountain trying to find some decorations for the table," he said. Pleased relief had broken through at last. His tone was light, mellow. "I'm preparing lunch. A lemon sole dish. Stuffed mushrooms. Why don't you go upstairs and lie down? Put a cold compress over your eyes. We'll call you in time for lunch. Dempsey, you come with me. That's a good boy." With Dempsey following, Randall padded off in his slippers while Deborah climbed the stairs, desperate to be alone, her stomach turning at the thought of lemon sole.

Bea and Randall stayed until early evening. Deborah thought they would never leave, yet, waving them off from the circular drive, she regretted not asking them to spend the night. Only loneliness waited back in the house, and she had had enough of that to last a lifetime. She stood a long time beneath the canopy of friendly stars before the cold night air drove her inside.

Closing the front door, she stood in the foyer listening to the sound of loneliness echo about the silent, spacious house. Now that she needed it so badly, her house did not feel like a sanctuary at all. There was a quality about its silence that was alienating. She felt a stranger in the rooms she had designed and furnished with the treasures from her family.

How was she to survive all alone? What would she do to occupy tomorrow and all day Sunday? She thought she had lived through the last of the weekends like the ones coming. What had she done then to endure their emptiness? There had always been Bea and Randall, but now neither of them could offer consolation about Dan. In those days there had been other men, but she had turned down so many invitations during the past months that everybody thought she was out of circulation. Other than Bea, she had never made a close woman friend, someone to call in times like these.

Why hadn't Dan called? Would he permit her to walk away from him just like that? If he cared for her, he wouldn't just let her go, not after all they had meant to each other. Surely he wouldn't. But he had to, Deborah sobbed on the way up the stairs to bed. He had to.

She slept mercifully late Saturday and was awakened by Dempsey scratching on the bedroom door to be let out. "Oh, Demps, you poor thing!" she cried, pulling on a robe and following his bounding form down the stairs to the back door. It had snowed during the night. The weather had not held after all. She wondered if Dan had left Phoenix yesterday for Denver. He would have been slowed because of bad driving conditions and forced to stop at a motel along the way. In which case, he would get into Denver around noon.

Deborah was suddenly sure that was what he had done. Her spirits lifted at once. With an eye on the clock, she went upstairs to wash and dry her hair in record time, brushing it out to bounce gloriously on her shoulders. She forsook the usual Saturday morning jeans and sweatshirt for mauve wool slacks and sweater, and by noon she and the house were as tidy as could be. Dempsey lay in the foyer by the door, having sensed an impending visitor.

But Dan did not come.

In the late afternoon she could bear the mocking silence of the house no longer. She needed the company of people and the sound of human voices. "I think I'll go to the mall, Demps. Want to go with me?" she invited. In the garage, the presence of Dan's Bronco was something of a comfort. One of these days he would have to come back to at least take possession of it. And she would still see him from time to time on the job site. As the architect in charge, she had every right to be there, especially during the crucial times of pouring concrete and erecting steel. She would certainly be at the site the day the steel columns went up. They represented a dream coming true, and she had been a part of it.

At the mall, congested with after-Thanksgiving shoppers buying for Christmas, Deborah allowed herself to be swept along in the crowds, barely conscious of anything but the growing ache in her heart and the continual mist in her eyes. Where was he? Why hadn't he called? What was he feeling, thinking? Was he in pain, too? Wandering into a movie, she left halfway through it. Two hours had passed. Two never-to-be-regained hours. She was furious with herself. She was quicker to waste money than time, and rarely did she do either. Her heels clicked on the pavement as she walked determinedly to the car where Dempsey waited, his large head stuck out the window, watching the passersby.

She would go home and eat a bite, then work on several preliminary designs in the studio. No more feeling sorry for herself. No more wasting time! She would work, work, work! That was the only antidote, the only solace, the only sure remedy for all pain, all grief. If Dan were as miserable as she, he would have called by now. Of course, there was the possibility that he would telephone tonight. Or that he had tried while she had been gone. What had he thought when she wasn't there? The car shot toward the foothills.

Making the circular drive around to the garage, she pressed the electronic door opener. The double door slid up, and a cry that had no breath behind it died in her throat. For a few frozen seconds, her mind refused to believe what her eyes so clearly saw. Dan's Bronco was gone! A white piece of paper had been taped to the service room door. Scrambling out of the car, Deborah snatched it down. *Deborah*, the bold, black writing ran, *your garage door was open when I came out with my construction superintendent to pick up the Bronco. Burglar bars won't help that kind of carelessness. Thanks for keeping the car. Dan.*

Deborah held the note to her breast. It was written on the same kind of memo paper as the other note from Dan, the one containing a circle shaded black. Dempsey began to whimper as he saw the tears start to trickle down the face of his mistress. Following her into the kitchen from the garage, he sat down on his haunches and waited patiently when she crumpled beside him and buried her face in his thick, black ruff.

Within the three-week period that the construction documents were in the hands of the zoning commission, Deborah conducted her personal and professional affairs in a trance, walking quietly through her days as if she were in a house of death. She had neither seen nor talked with Dan a single time since his return to Denver. She knew he was busy with the final preparations for beginning construction once the plans were approved. No doubt they filled his time, his heart, his mind; gave him comfort and relief—if he were in need of that.

"Now, Deborah," said Randall in her office the day before the plans were to be released, "I expect you to wear something

155

smashing for the ground-breaking ceremony and luncheon that follows. It's scheduled for the day after tomorrow, remember. All the local networks will be televising it as part of the evening news. The governor and mayor will be there. I will, too, of course, but the spotlight will be on *you*, the designer of the project."

"You forgot Dan," Deborah said dryly. "I imagine part of that spotlight will be on him too since it's his project. Will any other members of the corporation be attending?" If so, she hoped Clayton Thomas would not be among them.

"I'm not sure. As for Dan, I didn't wish to bring up an unpleasant subject. Have you, uh, seen him?"

Deborah continued to concentrate on the report of a site analysis she was writing. "Not since I saw him in Phoenix."

She could feel the beam of his smile. "All for the best, I'm sure. I am proud of you, my dear."

The intercom buzzed. "For you," Deborah said, handing Randall the phone, and went back to the report.

"What! What's that you say, Bea? Well, he could have informed us, the...ill-bred..."

Startled, Deborah looked up. She'd seldom heard Randall raise his voice. He ignored her interrogating gaze and snapped, "Cancel my appointments this afternoon, Bea, and I don't want to be disturbed once I come back to the office. I have some phone calls to make." He slammed the phone down with such fury that Deborah thought Bea's eardrum must be broken.

"What on earth—?" she queried.

"A friend of mine from the zoning office called to say that the Cutter Street plans were approved yesterday. Dan Parker picked them up—" He broke off, thinking hard.

Puzzled, Deborah stared at him. "But, that's wonderful! That means Dan can order the steel two days early. I don't know why you're so upset, Randall."

"The Hayden firm should have been informed that the plans had been accepted. It was an insult, a slap in the face that Dan did not let us know. I—I had a celebration party planned."

"We can still have the party," Deborah said soothingly. "Dan probably hasn't had a second to call us since he picked up the documents. He's probably been in financial huddles, meeting with suppliers, ordering materials. You know how it is, Randall, when a complex of this size is getting under way."

"Deborah—" Randall had found his dignity. He took a deep breath to regain his composure. "Dan Parker should have had the courtesy to inform us personally that those plans had been accepted. This firm spent weeks of careful and steady effort on those documents and labored under enormous hardship, as you well know. I expected him, if not from good breeding at least from common courtesy, to have the decency to let us know." Randall slammed the door as he left.

But Randall's outraged sense of decorum could not quell the gladness bursting inside Deborah. How relieved Dan must be, how eager now to get that first nail driven! He must be congratulated. She dialed the number of the town house, letting the phone ring and ring should Dan just be coming up the walk, unlocking the front door. But there was no answer.

She hung up, all the joy that had filled her sails suddenly gone. Once more, with the feeling of being set adrift alone on a doleful sea, she bent to the report.

Deborah had begun taking Dempsey for a brisk walk just before bedtime. The exercise and sharp mountain air helped to lessen the day's emotional weariness and induce sleep. That evening, as she was walking with Dempsey down the short lane leading to the circular drive, a pair of powerful headlights turned into the lane and flooded over them. Turning, she was momentarily blinded by the glare and groped for Dempsey's collar as the dog growled low in his throat. The vehicle stopped, it's motor cut off. She caught a flash of silver and the brief outline of a tall figure when the door opened and slammed. Her heart almost stopped. From the darkness came a deep and wonderfully familiar voice. "Don't you think this nonsense has gone on long enough?"

"Dan!" she cried, leaping forward. "Oh, my darling!"

"Lady, what you've put us through!" he said, seizing her to his chest, where Deborah proceeded to sob uncontrollably, clinging to him as if he were a life raft about to capsize.

"I love you," she choked. "I love you! I love you!"

"I figured you did," Dan said, his voice husky with feeling. "You just needed some time to realize it."

Later when they lay entwined and at peace, Dan proposed, "Let's make a deal not to say anything more to rock this shaky boat, Deborah. Neither of us can afford it emotionally. I know I sure can't. I've nearly been out of my mind for the past three weeks and frankly, I'd just as soon hold off on any more serious discussions until after construction is well under way. I need my wits about me right now. Is it a deal?"

Deborah, her eyes closed, nodded contentedly. "It's a deal."

He stirred to prop up on an elbow. She could feel him peering closely. "Did you really mean what you said about your career?"

Her eyes opened. They wandered lovingly over the strong features, imprinting them in memory. "My career has been a cushion, Dan. It's supported me, softened the blow of a number of losses I've suffered in my life. It's been all I've ever had that I could rely on."

"Until now," he said and asked persuasively, "What kind of losses?"

"You said you didn't want to rock this shaky boat, remember? I don't either. Right now I just want to be happy together. Every moment is so precious." Softly, she ran her hand down his muscular bicep.

The muscle quickened beneath her touch. "Deborah," he groaned as his head sank to her, "don't talk as if we won't have forever."

Deborah chose not to tell Randall about the reconciliation with Dan. She could do without his comments, having enough qualms of her own about it. Not even Bea suspected the change in their status. When Dan telephoned the office, the calls were assumed to pertain to business.

The ground-breaking ceremony on Friday was blessed with dry, brisk weather, just right for the fur coats worn by the wives of the dignitaries attending. Construction had already begun on the site, but for the morning occasion, labor had been suspended. The workers in their hard hats sat grouped together on one of the recently poured foundation slabs, enjoying thoughts of the refreshment tables. An area had been cleared for two of them, one for the sandwiches and coffee and cake, the other to hold Champagne and canapés.

Indeed, the mayor and governor did attend. The mayor, to the accompaniment of whirring television cameras and popping flash bulbs, spoke of Deborah in sonorous tones. "At last we have emerging in the architectural community the presence of a young but commanding talent," he beamed a smile at Deborah, "who is returning us to the quiet yet astonishing beauty of the classical age."

Deborah, standing to his right in a teal blue coat, wondered if the man knew what he was talking about. She was relieved when he directed his effusive speech to Dan. "Here is a man," the mayor said of the builder, "who has never allowed the problems of business to overwhelm his humane and environmental concerns." He launched into the story of Dan's generosity in permitting the complex to be constructed around Fred's Paper Shack and Josie's Bar—"Preserving for us all," he concluded, "an integral part of Cutter Street, of downtown Denver, the likes of which we will never see again."

"Oh, my," John Turner said under his breath to Deborah as the gathering dispersed to the refreshment tables, "that bit of nicely-rendered hogwash should guarantee business through the year 2000. And the publicity certainly can't hurt your chances of winning an AIA Honor Award, which I'm sure you've already thought about."

"I have to be nominated first, John," Deborah reminded him, wondering if the engineer possessed any other color suit but brown.

"What's this you say?" inquired the mayor pleasantly, falling back to escort the pretty architect to the Champagne. His wife had already taken charge of Dan.

"Oh," explained John, "I was just telling my esteemed colleague here"—Deborah suspected a thorn beneath the rose—"that her design of the complex is liable to win an award given by the American Institute of Architects."

"How very splendid," he said. "I'll ask Randall to keep me informed. What a plum that would be for Denver, not to mention the Hayden firm."

Randall, who was always so enthusiastic about his clients' ground-breaking ceremonies, seemed listless and unexcited about the one hosted by the Parker Corporation. "He's not been himself lately," Bea told Deborah when she remarked about his distant manner and preoccupied air at the luncheon that followed. "I don't know what's the matter with him."

Deborah wondered if Randall had guessed that she and Dan Parker had reconciled when she had declined his invitation to spend Christmas Day with him and Bea. "I am entertaining out-of-town guests for Christmas," she had explained.

"Which guests?"

"No one you know." It was the truth. Alicia Dameron was coming with her agent, the kindly man Deborah had met at Thanksgiving and to whom Alicia was now engaged.

But if so, Randall had made no mention of his suspicions, and that kind of restraint was not typical of him. Deborah worried that he might be ill. He was nearly seventy now and had been looking unduly tired. At the luncheon, she looked down the table at him. He was usually so delightfully urbane and witty on these occasions. Today he looked drawn and contributed little to the conversation.

As Christmas drew near, Deborah resolved to tell Dan about the events of eight years ago as soon as the steel support columns had been erected. Their delivery was due the day after New Year's. Once the steel was delivered and the columns up, the worst of Dan's anxieties about the complex would be over. The union representing the workers for the major steel manufacturing companies did indeed plan to strike the first of January. The steel inventories of local supply companies were already drying up due to the demands of builders and contractors for their orders before the strike deadline. Dan was worried that somehow, someway, there might be a glitch in his order that would delay the project. She would wait until it was safely at the site and those columns bolted to the foundation before she told him about Roger. Then, if his judgment proved harsh, she would withdraw from the project, request that John take over as the architect in charge, and remove herself once and for all from Dan's life.

Until then, there was Christmas to think about. Alicia and her agent were flying in late the twenty-third to say for three days. Deborah had a number of festivities arranged, including a skiing trip to Winter Park, a nearby resort.

"Don't plan anything for Christmas afternoon," Dan told her one evening. "I have a surprise."

"Oh, you and your surprises!" Deborah laughed and hung a red tree ornament on his ear. They were decorating the Christmas tree, a seven-foot fir that filled the picture window. The night before, they had spent several mirthful hours selecting it, then came home to whittle its base to fit the stand. There had never been a Christmas tree in the picture window. Until now, the family tree ornaments had remained packed in their shipping crates stacked in the basement. Deborah had asked that Dan bring them up for her. Memories leapt out as she pushed back the protective wrappings and lifted the baubles from their tissue nests. Dan had sensed the poignancy in her mood.

"You never talk about them, you know," he said.

"Who?" she asked.

"You know who, Deborah. Your parents, that's who."

Deborah found a spot on the tree for the ornament in her hand. Then, careful not to step on the boxes with their fragile contents, she made her way to Dan, sitting at the dining-room table. He was attempting, unsuccessfully, to make order of a glittering tangle of icicles.

"Dan?"

"Yes, honey?"

"You know I love you."

"Uh-huh."

"I have something that I must tell you, before...we can discuss the future."

"I suspected you did, but I know better than to rush you, Deborah, especially since I'm not going anywhere."

"I...want to tell you after New Year's, once the columns are up."

"Suits me," he said incuriously, glancing up, his expression lightly mocking her seriousness. He reached for her hand when she continued to regard him gravely. "Whatever it is, Deborah, it will not affect the way I feel about you. Believe me." The blue eyes held hers steadily, and something strangely knowing glimmered in their depths. Deborah drew back a little, conscious of a chill sweeping her spine. In that instant, she thought she had read her secret in his eyes.

Dan's "surprise" arrived on two runners and eight legs Christmas afternoon. He had hired a driver with a team of two horses and a sleigh for a ride through the snow-covered countryside. He'd thought of everything. There were bells tied with red ribbons on the harnesses, thermoses of hot cocoa, and song books for carols. The memory of the sights and sounds and feelings of the outing—the clop of hooves down country lanes, the jingle of bells, the peals of laughter, the off-key carols, the companionship, the cozy warmth of blankets and cocoa, the biting air and fresh sun—made an incalculable gift. "One we'll cherish forever, Daniel, you dear boy," fluted Alicia, looking like a figure on a Christmas card in white ermine cloche and scarf.

It was only after the laughter and fun of Christmas were over and the new year had begun that Deborah remembered the moment with Dan at the dining-room table. It was then that she comprehended the meaning in the clear blue eyes.

Chapter Eleven

The steel columns had arrived. They lay near the foundation of the headquarters building, stacked beneath tarpaulins to protect them from the lightly falling snow. Deborah left to Bill Williams, the construction superintendent, the job of measuring the lengths and went to join Dan in the site trailer.

Wearing a dark, fleece-lined jacket, he was sitting at a desk poring over invoices when she entered. "Good morning," he said, looking up with a smile. "Coffee's on. Fresh pot."

"I want something else first," she said, bending to kiss him.

When they drew apart, Dan's admiring gaze swept over her face, lingering on the snow in her hair. "You're gorgeous," he said.

"Naturally," she agreed, smiling. "I'm in love. How are things going?"

"Right on schedule. So far, so good." Dan tilted back in his chair with a satisfied stretch, making the statement more to Bill, who was at that moment entering the trailer, than to Deborah. Behind him was a man from the steel fabricating shop who had come to direct the erection of the columns. They brought in frosty breaths and dark looks. "You fellows ready to put 'em up?" Dan asked.

Bill glanced at Deborah before answering. She was a fine

young woman. He liked her even if she was a woman in a man's profession, and he knew the boss was totally gone on her. He sure hoped she wasn't responsible for this fine kettle of fish. "Not hardly," he said flatly. "Them steel columns is at least four inches short."

Dan's chair hit the floor, surprise hoisting him out of it. "What!" he said incredulously. "They can't be!"

Bill threw the industrial tape measure in its steel case onto the desk. "That thing don't lie, boss. It says that every one of them columns measures nineteen feet, eight inches. They were measured three times. We're four inches short."

Fire in his eye, Dan confronted the steel fabricator. "Mr. Parker," the man protested before Dan could speak, "unless my memory has completely gone bonkers, the structural drawings from the Hayden firm called for nineteen-foot, eight-inch columns. I was standing right there when our shop drawings were drafted from them. I called out the figures for the columns myself. Also, the shop drawings came back from the architect approved."

"Well, we'll soon see who's responsible for this," Dan gritted, spinning around to pull out rolls of blueprints from pigeon holes above the desk. "Not that it will make a damn bit of difference to this mess. The damage is done."

Deborah, agape in a nightmarish immobility, stood with the coffeepot still in her hand. Dan's apprehensions had not been unfounded, after all, but never in her darkest imaginings had she considered a disaster of this magnitude. For a steel fabricator to cut these particular columns too short was like a surgeon accidentally cutting the aorta. The entire support system of the headquarters building, which the rest of the complex adjoined, depended on the twenty-foot columns. Due to their unique features, they could not be extended at either end. The columns would have to be reordered. Not only would that result in a delay in construction prohibitive in cost, but to make Dan's situation worse, this morning, as feared, the major steel unions had declared a strike.

Slowly, while the structural and shop drawings were unrolled on the desk, she managed to return the coffeepot to its heating element. Watching the men compare the two sets of blueprints, one of which would prove conclusively whether the fabricating plant or the Hayden firm was at fault, she knew that John's vertical dimensions would show no error. Although Tony had approved them, the fabricator's shop drawings, taken from John's specifications and from which steel is cut to order, would have to bear responsibility for the four-inch miscalculation. As the architect in charge, she was answerable for any error committed by any member of her team. But there was small consolation in knowing that she would be found blameless. Dan's terrible predicament remained.

Still, her heart skipped a beat as all three heads lifted at once and all eyes fastened on her. No one spoke. Then Bill said gravely, "The shop drawings show the height of the columns as nineteen feet, eight inches."

Deborah's attention was riveted on Dan. Her flesh tingled with a chilly forewarning of his next words. "John's read nineteen feet, eight inches, also," he announced, incredibly.

"That's impossible!" She gasped.

"See for yourself," Dan invited tersely, thrusting out the roll of blueprints.

Dumbfounded, Deborah rolled out the structural drawings and studied John's computations of the columns. Nineteen feet, eight inches. "It can't be possible," she whispered, staring at Dan. "The figures have been altered from the originals! They had to have been! Somebody, somehow, tampered with them and changed the computations before they were sent to the fabricator so that the shop drawings would call for columns four inches short!"

The silence was palpable in the small trailer. Deborah sensed the embarrassed shift of Bill's eyes to the window, the fabricator's intent concentration on the floor. Dan spoke evenly, a muscle jumping along his jawline. "You were working under enormous pressure, Deborah. Don't you think it is possible that you overlooked John's computations in the final check? You couldn't have re-computed every measurement."

"No!" she protested. "For heaven's sake, Dan! You know those columns are the most important feature of the design! I checked those figures a dozen times. When you picked up the construction documents, the structural drawings called for twenty-foot columns. I would bet my life on it!" Getting no response other than a doubtful stare, Deborah approached him and cried, "Don't you understand what's happened here? Somebody, somehow, altered John's drawings to delay the project or—or—" An idea hit her, deepening her sense of horror. "Or to discredit me as the architect in charge!"

The fabricator cleared his throat uncomfortably. "Uh, excuse me, Mr. Parker, but since there's nothing else for me to do here today, I'll just get on back to the shop. I sure am sorry about all of this." He stuck out his hand to Dan, who offered a tautlipped apology that he had thought his plant in error. "Oh, that's all right," the man assured him. "In these situations, the fabricator's always the first one to be thought at fault, not the architect. I wish I could say that we could get you a reorder on those columns, but our steel supply is just about depleted. Every builder in town wanted to get a jump on the strike. I'm afraid I couldn't even talk about a delivery date before two, maybe three months."

Dan accepted the information with stiff grace and thanked the man for coming out. Bill, with slumped shoulders and eyes averted from Deborah, retreated with the fabricator.

When the door had closed, Dan demanded, "Do you know what you just did? News of this will spread fast enough, but you gave that fabricator quite a story to tell when he gets back to the shop! My God, Deborah, just admit the error and take the consequences. Don't make matters worse by denying responsibility for it!"

"Dan, you've got to believe me for your own sake," she pleaded desperately, clutching the front of his jacket. "Somebody deliberately and maliciously altered John's drawings to damage you financially or destroy my career—maybe both. I have a terrible feeling that someone in the firm is responsible. I don't see how this thing could have been successfully pulled off otherwise."

Dan jammed his hands into the pockets of his jacket and said, fighting to control his inner rage and disappointment, "Now, who would want to do that? Who in the firm could afford to go to such elaborate trouble to injure you professionally, Deborah? What would be the point? And as for damaging me financially by delaying the project, that could have been done without involving you or the Hayden firm. So that brings us back to you. Who would go to such nasty lengths to discredit you?"

Deborah thought immediately of John Turner. He wouldn't hesitate to bring her down any way he could, but not at the expense of the Hayden firm. "I—I don't know," she stammered in confusion, "but somebody did."

Dan regarded her in skeptical silence, bleak eyes betraying his disappointment in her. "You don't believe me, do you, my darling?" she stated in a small, lost voice, daring to place her hands on his mountainous shoulders.

"Don't you think I want to?" he said desolately. "Don't you think I know that more is at stake here than this project or your career? But right now the only certainty I know is that if I don't get another order of that specially rolled steel in here within the next week, I'm on the brink of financial ruin. Who did what to whom and who's responsible for what is the least of my concerns at the moment. I suggest you get back to the office and inform Randall of what's happened. Tell him to line up his attorneys. He'll be needing them if I know Clayton Thomas."

"Oh, no." Deborah breathed woefully. "He's still a member of the corporation?"

"Yes," Dan said shortly.

"Dan...I'm being...framed. That's the only word for it. I don't know why, but I am. John's original drawings of the columns showed them to be twenty feet in height the morning I turned them over to Randall to be printed for you to take to the zoning commission."

"Then the thing for you to do is get back to the office and check John's originals. If they show evidence of having been tampered with, then you'll have a case. It also means that somebody in the firm is responsible. The tampering had to have been done before the prints were made that I picked up on the twenty-second."

"And if there is no evidence of tampering?"

Dan contemplated the amber eyes, as clouded as a sunless autumn day. Closing his hands around hers, he clasped them tightly. "I don't know, Deborah. I just don't know."

Chilled from more than the near-freezing temperature, Deborah sailed past Bea into the production room to the flat file. All original drawings were stored in these drawers. Her hands were shaking by the time she located the ones she sought. Carefully, closely, she examined the mylar sheets with their pencilled lines. No doubt remained in her mind. With only a rubber-tipped pencil, someone had erased John's original figures and substituted others that altered the vertical dimensions of the columns by four inches. But there was not a telltale trace to prove it. Her blood ran cold. Who hated her enough to do this? Who wanted to malign her reputation, stop the project, bring Dan to the edge of financial ruin? Who? She took the drawings with her to Randall's office.

He was standing at a window looking out at the snow, hands clasped behind his back. "Randall?" The face he turned to her was that of a very tired, depleted old man. Lines that she had never seen before etched the pale, delicate skin. "You've heard, haven't you?" she said, shocked by his appearance.

"Heard what, my dear?"

Then he must be very ill, she thought, pierced by a cold dismay. She approached the desk, holding the drawings. "I think you'd better sit down, dear," she suggested gently. "I have some bad news."

"Oh? What kind of bad news?" Carefully, as if his fragile frame might break, Randall eased himself into the desk chair. "Come, come. Spill it out," he said when she hesitated. "Surely it can't be that bad."

But by the time Deborah had related the details of the morning's discovery, leaving out her suspicions about the alteration, Randall's mouth hung slack. "Oh, dear me, Deborah. This is indeed bad news." He stared off into space blankly, every now and then blinking as a consequence of the error was fully realized. Finally, he drew a deep breath and straightened resolutely. "We have weathered storms before," he said. "We'll ride this one out. Are those John's drawings?"

"Yes," she said hesitantly.

"Give them to me. I'm sure you realize that you will be removed as the architect in charge. The Parker Corporation will insist on it." He gave her the briefest of smiles. "You are still my child, Deborah. The Hayden firm is still your home. You're not about to be booted out, so have no fear of that. Neither is John. You are neither one to blame. It is the fault of that ridiculous deadline. Dan Parker, constructing a project of that enormity in the face of strikes and volatile interest rates, forcing us to work down to a gnat's fanny, is responsible for debacles of this kind. Businessmen never learn." He rose from the desk. "Give those to me," he said again, "and I'll go down and break the news to John."

"Randall—" Deborah held on to the documents, biting her lip.

"Yes, Deborah? What else is troubling you?"

"I think John's figures of the columns were deliberately altered after they left my office on the twenty-second. When I turned the structural drawings over to you, the height of the columns read twenty feet. They were changed some time that day before they were printed for Dan."

Alarmingly, Randall's face seemed to drain of every vestige of color, but the truth compelled her to press on. "It was done to discredit me or to ruin Dan financially, maybe even to cast a shadow on the Hayden firm. The purpose of the perpetrator could have been a combination of all three."

Slowly, Randall lowered himself back into his seat, jarred by her words. "What in the world are you saying, Deborah? That John altered his own drawings to blacken your reputation? I'm aware that you two have never gotten along, but he wouldn't do that!"

Deborah shook her head. "I'm convinced he wouldn't either. I'm not accusing John. He thinks too much of you to harm me at the expense of the firm, so I've discounted him as a possibility."

Randall blinked at her incredulously. When at last he spoke, his voice was sorrowful. "Deborah, my dear, you were under enormous pressure after the theft of your drawings. Don't you think that in those last days when time became so critical, you could have overlooked a mere four-inch miscalculation in his figures?"

"Well, there is one way to find out," said Deborah. "Let's get John in here. If he says his drawings have been altered, will you believe me?"

Randall gave that a moment's consideration. "I'm not saying John would, but he'd have every reason to lie in his own behalf. He would be in the clear if he supported your assertion. Did anybody else check his figures of the columns?"

"No, there wasn't time."

"Then allow me to go down to his office before this discussion goes any further. You stay here. You know how defensive he gets around you. I'll bring him along in a minute when I've explained what's happened."

Left alone, Deborah's worries turned from her own problems to Dan's. She prayed desperately that he could locate another supply of steel and that it could be rolled, fabricated, and delivered to the site within a week. She wouldn't allow herself to think about the ramifications if he couldn't. The site would have to be shut down, and that would trigger a chain reaction affecting everybody connected with the project, from stockholders to Fred and Josie, whose businesses could not really resume until construction was completed. And as for her and Dan...In searing anguish, she thought of how they had parted without a loving embrace, a kiss, an assurance of love. He wanted to believe her. She knew that. He had been as shocked, as disappointed in her denial of the error as he was about the error itself. She couldn't blame him from recoiling from what sounded like a cock-and-bull story. Of course she couldn't. But, oh, please God, let her be proved guiltless!

Her distraught musings broke off as the door opened, admitting Randall and a more than usually glum-faced John Turner. She stood up, fearful of what she discerned in their expressions. Randall spoke without preamble, verifying her fear. "John says that he computed the height of those columns at nineteen feet, eight inches, Deborah."

Round-eyed, Deborah gaped at the structural engineer. He said bleakly, "I'm sorry, Deborah. I really am. I was in such a rush—I got behind and I—I counted on you to catch any errors. You—you're so good at that—" Nervously, he ran his tongue over his lips. His voice cracked as he tried to continue. "Forgive me. I'm sorry." Reddening, he dropped his eyes from her incredulous stare.

"John—?" Deborah put out a hand to touch his arm. "Why are you lying? You know that you made no error in the vertical dimensions. Why would you say that you did?"

John did not answer. Eyes still averted, mouth clamped tightly, he seemed about to explode with some profound, private grief. A string of retorts formed on her tongue. She wanted to remind him that the truth would make no difference to her outcome. As the architect in charge, she was still responsible. Her career would still be severely damaged, a development that should please him. So why couldn't he tell the truth? Did he hate her so much that he couldn't bear for her to have even that small comfort?

But something in his remorse stayed her words. She turned away from him and sought a chair blindly. Randall said, "You may go back to your office now, John. I'll talk with you later."

When he had gone, Randall said somewhat brusquely, "You, too, should go back to your office, my dear. The press will hear about this shortly. I want you to answer no telephone calls, respond to no inquiries. I'll have to get in touch with our lawyers, line up our ducks. One further suggestion: Keep this theory of yours to yourself. It will serve only to discredit you further in the eyes of the architectural community."

Back at her desk, Deborah clasped her head in dismay. She had to be dreaming this insanity! What was going on here? Who had engineered this horror? Not John. Somehow she could not believe that John had altered his own computations to injure her, no matter how much he disliked her. But somebody in the firm had to be responsible. Only someone with a knowledge of in-house routine could have known, for instance, that when the shop drawings were returned to the firm for approval before the steel was cut, it would fall to Tony Pierson to check them for inaccuracies. He would do this by comparing them to the already modified structural drawings in the flat file. Since the two sets agreed, he would return the shop drawings to the steel fabricator as approved. If she or John had checked them, the discrepancy would have been spotted immediately and corrected.

Deborah tried to take a deep, calming breath, but anxiety bound her chest. And inevitably, one of the dreaded headaches was beginning its painful rhythm in her temples.

"We plan to sue this firm for every cent it's worth!" announced Clayton Thomas dramatically the next morning, relishing the rush of color that swept Deborah's coldly beautiful face.

"Now, hold on, Clayton—" interrupted Dan from his position by the window.

"No, you hold on!" snapped Thomas, redirecting his fury to the tall man who had preferred to stand during the meeting with the firm's attorneys in Randall's office. "From the very

beginning I was the only one of the five of us opposed to the se-
lection of *that woman*," he jabbed a finger at Deborah, "as the
designer of this project. Now I'm entitled to say I told you so.
Furthermore, I intend to see that this firm is held responsible
for any and all costs that accrue as a result of her incompetence.
I hope your insurance is current, Randall."

"Indeed it is." Randall did not seem to be in the least per-
turbed. "Deborah, would you care to be excused? There's no
reason for you to stay to listen to this diatribe."

"Thank you, Randall, but I prefer staying. Mr. Thomas has
every right to be upset."

"Not as upset as you're going to be, young lady, once word of
your monumental bungling reaches the ears of the building industry. You'll be lucky to get a commission to design outhouses!"

Deborah caught a whiff of Dan's cologne as he strode past
the back of her chair to the door. Opening it, he said decisively,
"Deborah, I want you to leave. Randall is right. Let the lawyers
handle this. Nothing can be gained from your presence here."

Without further argument, Deborah nodded, careful not to
meet Dan's eye when she walked past him out into the reception
room. They had not spoken since she left the job site yesterday
morning. She knew he had been too busy to call; his line had
been busy each time she'd dialed. But she had thought he would
get in touch with her some way. All night, as she lay awake listening for the sound of the Bronco in the circular drive, fear had
mounted that Dan now held her responsible for the disaster.
He'd had time to appreciate the full extent of her error and had
found that he could not forgive her its consequences. She'd been
shocked to find him already in Randall's office for the meeting.
She'd expected him to come by her office first.

The door closed behind her with a click of finality, bringing
a sense of loss so acute Deborah thought she might double over

from pain. Thankfully, Bea was out of the room. She could not have endured her well-meaning but ineffectual ministrations.

"Deborah?" Dan spoke directly behind her, causing her heart to jump. "Here," he said, unsnapping what sounded like a key from a ring. "This is to the town house. Meet me there after work. I may be a little late, but wait for me. Will you promise to do that?" The key was handed over her shoulder.

Deborah nodded mutely and accepted the key without turning. The door opened, then clicked again.

At five o'clock, Deborah was sitting in the dusk-shadowed living room of the town house. It had been a devastating day for her, but at least something of the Cutter Street debacle had been salvaged. Randall had saved the commission for the firm by the simple expedience of removing Deborah as the architect in charge and reassigning himself. New structural drawings had been ordered with Randall himself overseeing every specification. They would go to Dan in record time. He and Dan had convinced Clayton and the other less vindictive members of the corporation to hold off on a lawsuit until there was, in fact, a delay in construction. In the building schedule, Dan had wisely allowed a five-day grace period for the unexpected and unforeseen problems that can occur on any job site. There was a possibility that he could get another order of steel delivered within ten days, which would cut his losses considerably. And if the Parker Corporation did sue, Randall had assured Deborah that the firm was sufficiently insured to handle the financial damages.

Now that the smoke had begun to clear, it seemed to Deborah that she alone had taken a direct hit. Some giant hand had destroyed her life, her future—before her very eyes. Whatever tomorrows she might have shared with Dan would never be. Her oversight nearly cost him millions, and he believed she lacked the integrity to take the responsibility for her mistake. That, compounded by the knowledge of Roger's death, would surely destroy the love Dan felt for her.

And the damage to her career, although a secondary loss in comparison to her greater grief, would be irreparable. Never again would she enjoy the esteem, the respect, the trust of associates and clients as she had in the past. Even if she discovered whose hand had changed those computations, the injury had been done to her reputation. Just as there was no returning to the love that she and Dan had known.

And the firm would no longer seem like a loving family. She felt an outsider now, estranged from the group. One of its members had maliciously tried to destroy her life, and until she found out which one, she would suspect them all, even Bea, who—Lord forbid—could well have harbored a grudge against her all these years.

Deborah sighed in weariness as the telephone jarred her already tense nerves. Probably that was Dan, calling to see if she were there. The caller was not, however. A rough male voice demanded abruptly, "Let me speak to Bear Parker. This is his old buddy at the Lanscomb Steel Company in San Antonio, Texas. I'm Harvey Lanscomb."

"Who?" she said, dumfounded. "Who did you say?"

"Harvey Lanscomb. I need to talk with Bear Parker, pronto, miss. Is that boy around?"

Bear—Bear—Bear. She was catapulted back into the past, to the night Roger had picked up a letter from the floor.

"Lady, are you his secretary?" the man demanded. "I need to locate him, or at least leave a message. Hello? Are you there?"

"Yes. Yes, I'm here." Deborah spoke through the fire in her throat. "What is the message?"

"Tell him that his old buddy came through for him. Tell him I've got his steel and will have it on the job site in six days, if we can get some structural specifications down here. Got that?"

"I—I've got it," Deborah could barely whisper. "Indeed I do." She was remembering Roger's delighted grin, the way he had glanced up from the letter and explained that it was from Bear, his best man.

"Tell him to call me when he gets in. Here's the number in case he doesn't have it handy."

Her hand was shaking badly, and her heart threatened to pound through her chest, but Deborah managed to write down the man's name and number. "Is that all?" she asked.

"How is that old son of a gun anyway?" the man asked heartily. "Bear and I go back a long way, all the way to Lawsonville, Virginia, our hometown. Bear is his nickname. Got it playing football 'cause he looked like one and played like one back in those days. He use that handle out there?"

"No," Deborah answered. "He doesn't use that name here."

"You his girlfriend? I wouldn't figure he'd have his secretary at his house. Or maybe he would." A hearty chuckle followed.

"I'm neither," she said. "I'll leave Mr. Parker your message."

"Oh, yes, well, you be sure and do that, young lady," Harvey Lanscomb said in embarrassment, realizing he might have made a tactless remark. "Bear sure does need this steel."

Deborah hung up in a haze of grief. Yes, indeed, he needed that steel. It had probably been ordered at the same time as the other and held until Dan had wreaked his vengeance. *Oh, my darling, you gave me a dozen clues, and I never saw one!*

She left the key on a hurriedly written note, addressed to Bear, by the telephone, then quickly put on her coat and fled the town house. She must go to Randall—to her usual port in a storm.

"Good heavens!" he exclaimed when he opened his door a half hour later. "What's happened now? You look pale as death!"

"Randall, it was Dan!" Deborah burst out. "Dan had the plans altered!"

"What? Dear child, come into the library where it's warm, and let me get you some brandy. Sit there by the fire. Now tell me slowly what you're talking about."

Deborah swallowed, struggling to gain possession of herself. When Randall returned with the brandy, she took a quick swallow and made an effort to speak intelligibly. "You remember the tragic story I told you of Roger Lawson, my former fiancé, and his mother, Estelle?"

"Of course I do," murmured Randall.

"At Thanksgiving, Alicia told me a tragic story about Dan. It seems that when she first knew him, he was heartsick over the death of a friend he had known since childhood, a man who had been killed in a car accident. His mother, who had helped to raise Dan, died from apparent grief shortly afterward. This happened eight years ago, at the same time that I—" Deborah used the term that Dan would have chosen, "*jilted* Roger and caused his death."

Randall, stupefied, asked, "Are you saying that Dan's best friend was Roger?"

"Dan was to have been Roger's best man. I never met him and had only heard him referred to as *Bear*. Now I recall that...that Bear was a builder. He was out of the country when Roger and I were engaged and was to have flown in for the wedding."

Randall's pale eyes had deepened with shock. "And did you determine that Dan is Bear?" he asked.

Deborah related the substance of the telephone call. "The

whole thing was very carefully executed from the beginning," she said, getting up to pace. If she kept moving, her blood would flow. If she sat down, everything inside would freeze. "First, Dan made sure the Hayden firm was awarded the bid for the complex. I don't know exactly how he did that since we didn't submit a bid until after we found out that he had bought Josie's and Fred's block. But that's a minor detail. I'll figure that out later."

"Maybe he had followed your career so closely that he knew how fond you were of them?" Randall suggested.

"Could be," Deborah agreed. "Certainly he has followed my career. The next thing he did was to engineer an affair with me." She blushed as she said it, her heart ripping in two. "Once that was under way," she continued, "he suggested a Saturday outing, one in which we would be gone all day, and *asked me to bring along Dempsey*. That move assured that the man he hired to steal the drawings would have clear entry into my house."

"And for what purpose did he steal the drawings, Deborah?"

"To put me under even more pressure so that it would be easier to believe I had overlooked an error in the computations."

"But—but—" Randall looked bewildered. "How did he know John would make an error in the computations?"

"Oh, Randall, don't you see?" Deborah stopped her pacing to look askance at him. "Dan hired John Turner to alter the drawings! That's why John lied about them yesterday. He altered them after the final check. Don't you see?"

"Yes, yes, I believe I am beginning to see everything," Randall said slowly. "As punishment for what you did to Roger— since your career destroyed his best friend—Dan would see to it that he destroyed your career. But wouldn't the cost to him financially make such an elaborate vengeance prohibitive?"

Deborah scoffed bitterly. "Oh, you can bet Dan Parker did

not invest more than he could afford. That supply of steel waiting in San Antonio will cut his losses, and the lawsuit he'll bring against the firm will offset the rest. Dan won't be out a penny for any of these machinations."

"We'll see about that," Randall said emphatically and got to his feet. He seemed relieved, as if a great weight had been lifted from his frail shoulders. "You must stay here tonight," he said, taking charge. "You can't go home with that madman roaming about. I'll go get Dempsey and bring him here. He shouldn't stay out overnight in this kind of weather. While I'm there, I'll pack a bag for you. No, don't bother about giving me your keys," he said when she went for her purse. "I have the set you gave me when you went to Phoenix for Thanksgiving. I keep forgetting to give them back." He leaned over to kiss her pale cheek, smiling fondly. "My dear girl, don't worry. I will protect you, as always."

When Randall had gone, Deborah sat down before the fire and stared into the flames. She felt in the grip of a deeply penetrating cold, the kind of cold that lies at the heart of betrayal, which no warmth would ever reach. *Dan...Dan...* She had thought him a mountain, heroic. From the beginning, she should have seen the clues. No man had ever looked at her the way Dan did the first time they met. He had not looked—he had studied. And always, every time she approached the subject of Roger, she had sensed a stillness in him, as if he were holding his breath expectantly. The morning the falcon was shot he had asked, "Is that all of the story?" intimating there was more, observing her with that puzzling scrutiny. Other memories came out of the flames; scenes, comments that she had heard and seen through the senses of love. The one of Mrs. Watson reporting a framed photograph missing. Dan claimed that it had been broken. Now she knew that it must have been a picture of

181

Roger. The night they reconciled: *My career has been a cushion, Dan…all that I've ever had that I could rely on.* "Until now," he had said. Now she understood the chilling awareness that had been in those blue eyes the night they decorated the Christmas tree: "Whatever it is, Deborah, it will not affect the way I feel about you. Believe me."

She should have believed him. He had told her the truth. Her head began to pound with one of the familiar headaches. She must lie down. Forcing herself to rise, she walked into the guest room. It was so cold in here. Where would Randall keep guest blankets? In the old-fashioned cedar chest at the foot of the bed, like the old-fashioned gentleman he was. She moved to the chest and lifted the lid.

What she saw on top of the blankets made her gasp. The room began to spin. Her mind stopped working. She stood frozen, staring down at the contents. Inside the cedar chest was her stolen mink coat.

Chapter Twelve

When her mind thawed enough to function, Deborah's first thought was that there had to be some mistake. This *couldn't* be her coat, the one that had belonged to her mother—the one stolen along with the drawings and other things that Saturday in September. But then she lifted the coat out of the chest, recognized its cut and feel, the faint fragrance of her perfume even before checking the monogram sewn inside. The right side felt heavy. From the pocket, she drew out the gold chain and diamond-and-pearl earrings described on the police list of stolen articles.

Before allowing herself to think the unthinkable, Deborah briefly considered the possibility that Randall—ever caring and thoughtful Randall—had somehow chased down the stolen articles, knowing how much they meant to her, and planned to present them next month on her thirtieth birthday. But then she saw the framed picture of herself that had been stolen. What pawn shop—what *fence*—would have kept such an item to sell?

Deborah dropped the coat and pressed her temples to steady the whirling floor. What was Randall doing with her things? He loved her—like a father. She was sure of that. But the fact that these items were here meant that he had stolen them, and why would he want to do that? To possess something intimate and personal of hers? But if all he had wanted were these things, why had he taken the drawings? Because if Randall had stolen them, then that meant that Dan—*that Dan had not*!

"Oh, my dear," said Randall in annoyance from the doorway, "what have you discovered? I am quite surprised at you. Didn't your parents ever teach you that it is impolite to rummage through other people's closets and cupboards? Dempsey, watch your feet!" he commanded the big Labrador as the dog rushed to greet his mistress.

Deborah stared at the figure of her mentor as a series of whole new theories began to jostle around in her brain. He looked so harmless, endearing really, muffled in the plaid scarf, one end hanging to his knee. Cheeks and nose were wintry red above it, and his hair and brows, all fleecy white now, stuck out from beneath the brim of an old-fashioned golfer's cap. He needed only knickers to look as if he had stepped out of a Currier and Ives lithograph.

Struggling to remain calm, to think clearly in spite of the hammer blows of the headache, Deborah bent down to embrace the cold, ruffled neck of the dog, grateful beyond measure for his familiar company. Something dictated that it was absolutely essential to appear composed. "I was looking for a blanket and found these things," she answered with equanimity. "What are they doing here?"

Randall did not reply. He removed the scarf and cap and held them for a moment, considering her thoughtfully. Then he said, "Let's go into the library where it's warm. I could do with a cocktail. What may I get you?"

"A couple of aspirin."

"Very well. Kindly take Dempsey into the library."

Moments later Randall joined them with a bottle of aspirin. He shook out several into Deborah's palm and handed her a glass of water that he had poured from the bar. "That should do the trick," he said, watching her swallow the tablets. "May I feed Dempsey before our chat? What I have to say may take some time. I brought his food, and he's hungry."

"All right," Deborah agreed, easing her head back against the chair. A gradual warmth was beginning to penetrate the numbness. If Dan had not stolen the drawings, then could that mean that he had not hired John to alter the structural documents? Could it be that he had no hand at all in any of this?

When Randall returned, he went to the bar and splashed scotch over ice in a glass of Waterford crystal. Bringing it to the fire, he remarked, "Another one of your headaches, my dear?"

"Yes. I had thought I was over them, but that, too, was a delusion. Why did you steal the drawings, Randall?"

"Now, my dear," he flinched, "do not use such harsh terms to describe my actions. After all, I am your mentor, your confidant, the one who put you back together eight years ago, the one who took a chance with you, nurtured your talent, molded you, developed you. In short, created you."

Deborah brought her head up. A light had just been shed on this mystery. "In other words, you are my Pygmalion and I your Galatea," she said, referring to the legend in which a sculptor fell in love with the statue he had created.

Randall chuckled delightedly. "Aptly put, my dear, aptly put. I had never thought of our association in those terms, but now that you put it in that perspective, I do believe you are right. Not that I am in love with you in any sexual sense, heaven forbid!" he exclaimed, casting his eyes upward.

Deborah gaped in amazement at the man she had revered and loved for so long. "You altered the drawings, didn't you?" she said as the pieces of the puzzle clicked rapidly into place. "Of course you did! You had ample opportunity, time, and certainly the knowledge. You knew the exact procedure, the precise status of those drawings every step of the way. But why, Randall?" she asked incredulously. "*Why?* Was it to destroy Dan financially? But that would mean destroying me!"

"*I*—destroy you?" The thought shocked Randall. "No! No! No! Don't you understand that I was trying to *save* you from a dreadful fate, preserve you for me, for the firm, for posterity. A gift like yours is rare, dear child. Your reputation may suffer a temporary setback, but talent will out, as they say. With the firm behind you, you'll resume your status in no time."

Dempsey ambled in to plop tiredly on the floor, and Deborah suddenly thought of something. "Oh, no!" she burst out, her laughter edged with hysteria.

"What is so amusing?" Randall frowned.

"Not amusing. Ridiculous. This whole mad business could have been avoided if I'd been able to pin down something that has been pestering my subconscious. It was a remark you made to me about Dempsey the morning I told you about the robbery."

"What was that?"

"When I mentioned that I was relieved that Dan had been with me, you said, 'Yes, thank goodness someone besides Dempsey was with you.' I didn't think about it at the time, assuming you were referring to the presence of Dempsey in the backyard. But now I realize that you knew he was with me in the car when we drove up to the house. You gave yourself away, and I didn't even see it."

"We never see what we're not looking for, child," he said. "My plan to relieve you of the drawings was made easier because you took the dear fellow with you. I learned of that intention when I monitored your telephone call from Dan earlier. But I had already made a trial run with Dempsey, so to speak, one evening when I was...well, *spying* isn't the most flattering of terms, but it will do...on you and Dan. I had to determine the exact nature of your relationship, don't you see. Anyway, I parked in the alley and walked to the back fence to see if the dog would take a tidbit, like the kind I intended doctoring with a sleeping tablet to put him out while I went about my business. I can't tell you how heartened I was to see Dan drive away that night. That's how I knew you'd had a good night's rest."

He gave her his slow, mellow smile and Deborah felt a clammy fear crawl along her backbone. When had insanity overtaken the brilliant faculties she had so admired? When had the creative energy sparkling in the pale blue eyes become the animation of madness? "How could you save me by trying to discredit me?" she asked, covertly looking around for her purse. She had to keep him talking until she could locate it since it contained her keys. "I assume the fate you saw for me was marriage to Dan?"

"Precisely. Marriages today are not what they used to be, Deborah. Devotion, fidelity, honesty—they are commitments of the past, like honor and quality. The inevitable aftermath of today's marriage is divorce, custody battles, ruination of the spirit, confidence, and talent. And as for children! Well! The modern child is little more than a monster. It is intellectually and physically lazy, undisciplined, indulged, and promiscuous. It has no mind, no heart. It runs on glandular secretions stimulated by television and fueled by soda pop and snack foods." Randall grimaced from the picture he had drawn. "You are my crowning achievement, dear child. I was not about to turn you over to *that*."

"You must have thought your plan divinely sanctioned when Dan turned out to be Roger Lawson's best friend," Deborah said, her lips lifting ironically. "A perfect candidate to blame for the destruction of my career."

"I wasn't trying to destroy your career, blast it!" Randall raised his voice. "You must understand that, Deborah! I thought that by having it appear that John had made an error you didn't catch, an error you would naturally deny and that would cost Dan heavily, a wedge could be driven between you. He would have to blame you. He could not possibly forgive you. You were not emotionally stable enough to handle his anger and lack of forgiveness. Your sordid association couldn't help but disintegrate. Had I known that you had come to your senses in Phoenix over Thanksgiving, I could have saved myself, and you, all this trouble."

Deborah watched him get up to replenish his drink, unusual for Randall, who never drank more than one cocktail before dinner. He was agitated, combustible. As for her, she could feel an almost euphoric cessation of the drumming within her head, as if the band were going home.

"By then, of course," Randall continued, "the altered drawings were already at the city planning and zoning office, but there was a way to retrieve them, I thought, with none the wiser about what had occurred. I made arrangements with an old friend of mine, an employee there who owes me a few favors, to call me once the documents were approved. I intended to pick them up, switch the altered drawings with correct ones, then give the packet to Dan during a little ceremonial party at the office to make the gesture seem more natural. The steel could then be ordered to the proper dimensions, and life would continue as normal."

"But the documents were approved two days early," Deborah mused, remembering the anger Randall had displayed when informed that Dan had already picked them up.

"Yes." Randall sighed. "My informant was out with influenza, unfortunately, and was unaware of what had occurred. By the time he called, the structural drawings were already on the way to the fabricator, and the die was cast. I couldn't issue a change order without implicating myself. I couldn't risk any record, anywhere, that might expose what I had done."

"You talked John into lying about the columns when you went down to his office yesterday, didn't you? He was never a part of this until then." Strangely, her words seemed to be coming from far away, as if her voice were in the other room.

"Yes. The dear boy would do anything for me, but then I also made him a handsome offer to ensure his loyalty."

"And what was that?"

"Why, I promised him your position as head of the urban planning department, my dear. You'll be moving into my office when I retire anyway, which will be shortly. However, he doesn't have to know that. Are you aware that you're still wearing your coat?"

"Yes," Deborah said, openly looking for her purse. She spotted it across the room on a Victorian settee. She had to get out of here. She would just rouse Dempsey, grab her purse, and go. She stood up, conscious that the room was assuming odd shapes and sizes. At the bar, Randall had suddenly thinned into a long, vertical figure that weaved grotesquely as if he were being reflected in a carnival mirror. She nudged Dempsey, lying in the center of the room, but the dog did not stir.

She stared accusingly at Randall. "You gave him something in his food! You—you gave him sleeping pills!"

"Yes," he said with a smile that broke across his face like a pencil line. "He gobbled them right down in the meatballs left over from Sunday's bridge party. We've missed your presence at them, Deborah. You'll have to start coming again."

"Never!" The declaration had the quality of a sound from a record played on a too-low speed. "I am leaving you, Randall. I am leaving the firm. You are insane, mad as a hatter. I love Dan. I will always love him. I can't think of anything in the world I would ever want more than to be his wife and to have his children." She groped for Dempsey's collar, keeping an eye on Randall, who stood weaving in amusement at the bar. "Come on, Demps!" she pleaded, tugging at his collar. "Come awake, boy!"

"Oh, I was so afraid you would feel that way, my dear. That is why I gave you sleeping pills, too. Now I must decide what to do with you once you are incapacitated." At her stricken look, he explained, "You belong to me, you see. I created you. Therefore, it follows that I have every right to destroy you. Don't be concerned for Dempsey. I've missed having a dog. He'll have a good home with me."

The ringing of the doorbell startled him, and Deborah seized that moment to propel her lethargic legs toward the open door of the library. "Help!" she screamed. "Help me!"

Randall hissed a crude imprecation and clutched at the tail of her coat. She whirled to flail at him, meanwhile grabbing her purse and hurling it with all her might at the double glass globes of a floor lamp. "Help!" she screamed again, pushing out the cry, hoping the caller had heard the shattering glass.

Immediately a pounding came at the door. Deborah heard Dan yell, "Deborah! Are you in there, Deborah?"

Joyous relief surged through her. "Dan!" she cried, desperately fighting the debilitating drowsiness and the thin circle of Randall's surprisingly strong arms as he pulled her back into the library.

Unexpectedly, he stumbled, falling backward with a curse over Dempsey's prone body, and she was free. Sobbing Dan's name, struggling like a swimmer caught in an undertow, she reached the door. Her fingers grasped the handle and fumbled with the intricate night latch. Randall, his breathing harsh, appeared behind her, grappling, vituperative, and violent. He struck at her just as the door opened, and a draft of cold, blessed air rushed in. Beneath the porch light stood Dan, tall and strong, a mountain of refuge. He reached for her, drew her to the safe shelter of his arms. "What the hell is going on here, Randall?" he demanded.

"He gave us sleeping pills," Deborah gasped. "Dempsey— Dempsey is still inside!"

It was morning when she awoke. A cold sunlight seeped through the snow patches on the windows of the bedroom, promising a fuller warmth later in the day. The smell of coffee drifted in from the door pushed open by an unseen visitor; a large canine head appeared at the foot of the bed. "Demps!" she cried with relief, rising up. "I am so glad you're all right!"

"Not nearly as glad as I am that *you* are all right!" said Dan, coming into his bedroom with a cup of coffee. Deborah thought that she must have died and gone to heaven. But no, the kiss planted on her lips by the man she loved was physical enough to warrant the belief that she was still alive. "Part of you is still in working order, at least." He grinned. "How do you feel?"

"Happy to be alive," Deborah said, taking the coffee. "To be here with you. How did you get us out of there last night?"

"I told Randall that after I put you into the Bronco, I intended to call my superintendent on the car phone to instruct him to call the police if he didn't hear from me in ten minutes. He was only too happy to let me in to retrieve Dempsey and your purse. You remember anything after falling into my arms?"

"Vaguely being walked around and forced to drink hot coffee."

"That was all they could recommend at the hospital. It was too late to pump out your stomach, which is just as well now. Your heartbeat and pulse were returning to normal, so the doctor thought you could be released into my care as long as I could keep you awake until it was safe to let you sleep."

"How did you know I was at Randall's?" Deborah asked, moving over so that Dan could sit beside her on the bed. Her spirits were soaring. She felt reborn into a world without migraines.

Dan rubbed her cheek with the back of his hand. "It was the only place you would have gone after you left my town house yesterday. My heart dropped to my knees when I got your note and then talked to Harvey. He told me all about his conversation with you, and I realized what you had to be thinking, how you must have been putting the pieces together but were still coming up with the wrong answers. By then I was positive that the drawings *had* been altered and that Randall was responsible. I saw his motive clearly. He was maniacally possessive of you. By altering those plans, he could cripple me financially, destroy our relationship, and tighten your ties to him. It's a magnanimous boss who doesn't fire an architect guilty of that kind of blunder. And in addition, now that he would learn of my association with Roger, he would even have me to blame for it! I would have been at Randall's sooner, but Bea paid me a little visit."

"Bea?" Deborah asked in surprise, remembering, now that she thought about it, that Bea had been out of the office most of yesterday. No one had known where she was.

"She was a very disturbed lady, torn between her loyalty and love for Randall and her affection for you. She came to

192

tell me that she suspected Randall of sabotaging the plans. She had no proof, just her feelings, but she said that recently he had increased the firm's liability coverage by an unusually large amount—too much of a coincidence, to her way of thinking, in the light of what has happened. Also, she said that he has been unlike himself since he got a mysterious call from the zoning office on the day the plans were supposed to have been approved."

"That's so," Deborah agreed, "and he did alter the drawings. He admitted it after I found my stolen things in a cedar chest in his guest room. "Yes," she said in response to the surprised hike of Dan's brows, "he was the thief who stole the architectural drawings."

"Well, I'll be…" Dan said, comprehension breaking across his face. He got up from the bed and tossed her his robe. "I'll get out of here and leave you to dress. See you in the kitchen in a few minutes, and we'll tie up the rest of the loose ends. It's time we had a long talk."

Presently, wearing the voluminous robe, Deborah joined Dan in the kitchen. He had placed milk and cereal on the table. She sat down at a bowl turned upside down on a plate. "Dan, I want to talk about Roger first."

"I do, too," he said quietly. "If we had only talked earlier, all of this could have been avoided."

"Why didn't you?"

Dan drew a chair close and sandwiched her small hands between his. Intently gazing into her eyes, he said, "I wanted to, honey. At first there was no point in bringing up Roger. It was obvious to me the day we met in the conference room that you did not recall my name in connection with him, so I thought, what does it matter? She never needs to know."

"But then, as we became involved and as I came to love you, I really didn't know what to do. It was clear you were still

193

hurting from the past, still felt guilty about it, still felt estranged from Savannah and the memory of your parents. I frankly was scared of what your reaction would be once you knew of my connection to Roger. I decided to wait until I was sure of your feelings for me before I said anything, and maybe in that time you'd come to me. After that bomb you dropped on me on Thanksgiving, I was terrified of losing you."

"Dan, dearest." Deborah kissed him softly, her eyes glimmering with tears. "Do you know the reason for that charade in Phoenix?"

Dan looked thunderstruck as she related Alicia's narrative. "Because the incidents were so similar," she concluded, "I couldn't risk telling you about Roger, not then. I couldn't have withstood your rejection, Dan. But I did intend to tell you," she said, wanting to make that clear.

"I know, honey. After New Year's. I wish you had believed me when I said that nothing would change the way I felt about you."

"But my parents' feelings for me changed, Dan. They never forgave me for what I did to Roger, to our family name. I couldn't imagine that you would forgive me."

"And what do you think you did, sweetheart?" He asked the question earnestly but kindly, holding her face between his hands. He asked again, "What do you think you did?"

"Why, I—I caused Roger's death."

"No, you didn't, my love. Roger had been drinking heavily. He was bombed out of his mind when he crashed into that wall, a fact that I'm sure Estelle omitted when launching you on this eight-year guilt trip. Sure, the broken engagement led to the drinking, but Roger has to bear the responsibility for that. Estelle blamed you because she could not afford to blame herself. Your parents were guilty of the same subterfuge. They

194

knew they were coercing you into marrying Roger. If they had permitted you your own life, Roger might be alive today. That was something Estelle and your folks could never bear to think about, so they let you carry their guilt. Roger himself admitted to me in letters that he knew you didn't love him. He knew he was taking advantage of a situation in which you had no voice. He justified his action by the fact that he truly loved you and believed that someday you would come to love him."

Tears began to spill over the two big thumbs stroking her cheeks. An ice floe was breaking up within her, pulling away from the banks, melting in the sudden flow of warm water. "You mean that I—that I'm not responsible for Roger dying?"

"Your courage in refusing to marry a man you did not love, not only for your sake, but for his, had a tragic consequence, honey, but that is the extent of your blame."

The joy of absolution flooded her soul. What would it be like to live without the guilt and pain that had been such a part of her life for so many years? But there was one final question. "Dan," she asked, staring into his eyes and holding on to his strong wrists, "did you...ever blame me?"

"No," he answered, blinking at a quick film of moisture. "The saddest day of my life was the day Roger was buried. I hurt for Estelle, whose only failing was meddling in other people's lives. She meant well, but this time it had tragic results. That was the way I saw it. Through the years, I wondered about the girl Roger had loved. If she was as sensitive and sweet as he thought she was, then I knew she had to be out there somewhere, carrying a mighty big burden. A few years ago, I picked up on your career. It was easy to follow from then on. I never intended—never even wanted—our paths to cross. We would just be painful reminders to each other. But then you submitted those renderings of the complex, and when I saw your concept of my headquarters, well, I knew I wouldn't even consider another designer." He bent forward, touching her forehead with his own. "And you know what?"

"What?" she whispered, the tears falling and splashing everywhere.

"Before the meeting was over that day in the conference room, the same feeling had come over me that I used to get in the jungles of South America when I'd read Roger's letters about you. I think I must have loved you even then."

"Dan..." She found it impossible to continue. What a long journey it had been for both of them, but it was over now. They had arrived. They were home.

"And now," he said, kissing her lightly, "if you'll just look under that bowl on your plate and give me an answer before I have to go to work for a few hours, I'd appreciate it. You and Demps stay here until I come in, then we'll go out to the foothills and get you some clothes. I think it's a good idea for you to stay with me for a while until we can settle this thing with Randall."

"We still haven't talked about him."

"There will be time, honey. There's always time to talk about the past. Now look under that bowl."

Still in the shelter of his arms, Deborah lifted the bowl. In the center of the plate was a blue velvet box. "I had that for you on Thanksgiving," Dan said, as very slowly, Deborah lifted the lid. Her mouth formed a soft *O* of surprise. She slipped the ring on her finger and looked at the man she would now be able to hold and cherish for the rest of her life.

"Yes," she said.

Epilogue

He could always turn around and go back, John Turner thought as he paused on the wide front step, the large coat box tucked under his arm. He looked back at the trail of his footsteps leading to the front of the house Deborah had designed ten years ago for her growing family. The falling snow was already obliterating the evidence of his arrival. If he left now, after a few minutes, no visible sign of his coming and going would remain.

He wished it were possible for time to have obliterated Deborah's memories of him the way that the snow was wiping out his footprints. How wonderful if the years had erased the memory of his treachery and left only the recollection of his name and face to the woman whose name and face had occupied his thoughts for years.

But she had landed on her feet, that was certain. In wry amusement, he thought how typical of Deborah Standridge to wind up with happiness, and he, the Hayden firm.

John moved up under the overhang and surveyed the snow-covered lawn, imagining it green and sweeping, a romping ground where Deborah's two sons played. There was a daughter, too; she must be three years old by now. It was hard to believe that Deborah herself had just turned forty.

He had seen her only three times in the past ten years, twice at a distance and once in the theater during intermission when she had stood so close he could have touched her. He had backed into the crowd, his heart wrenching at her stunning beauty. She had been on the arm of her tall, silver-haired husband, a vision in satin and sable, drawing all eyes. Hers had been on none but the distinguished man at her side.

She had never gone back to the Hayden firm once Randall had fired her, a surprise move that had stunned them all. So many had left the firm since she was there. Bea had defected immediately, another surprising blow. She had gone to work for Dan Parker and then, lo and behold, she had up and married his construction superintendent.

Most shocking of all, though, had been Deborah's marriage to Dan Parker. Everybody had thought it over between them, especially since Deborah was publicly blamed for nearly wrecking the project. If he had known then what he knew now, he would never have agreed to admit that he had computed those support columns four inches short.

Well, that was why he was here. He could never wipe the slate clean, but at least he could sleep better at night. He rang the doorbell. After a few minutes, the door was opened by a gray-haired woman in a maid's uniform. She stood in an anteroom separated from the foyer by an ornately grilled door through which he could see a sweeping flight of stairs. "Yes? May I help you?"

John handed her his card. "Good afternoon. I am John Turner. I wonder if I might see Mrs. Parker?"

Mrs. Watson's assessing gaze swept over the brown-coated figure before studying the card. "Does Mrs. Parker know you?"

"Yes, yes, she does, but she is not expecting me," John said. He indicated the box. "I have something for her, something that belongs to her."

After deliberating, Mrs. Watson invited him into the ante-room, and the door clicked shut as she went off to notify Mrs. Parker of her visitor.

He was kept waiting for only a few minutes before he saw Deborah, still beautiful—lovelier even—come down the stairs. He rose, clutching the coat box, as she opened the grilled door. "Hello, John," she said in the soft Southern voice he remembered so well. She did not extend her hand but stood aside and said, "Please come in. Let's go into the library where there's a fire."

It was, of course, a magnificent house, but homey and comfortable, full of family life. Deborah collected a doll and several other toys from a sofa by the fireplace, saying, "My daughter likes to play here. Do sit down, John. You'll find this spot comfortable." She sat opposite him, making no offer to give him tea or to take his coat. "Mrs. Watson tells me that you have something that belongs to me."

"Well, uh, yes, Deborah." He spoke for the first time, his heart beating rapidly. "I know you would want these things since your home burned down the day you...left the firm. I regretted the loss of the heirlooms you treasured so highly." He handed her the box. "I am the executor of Randall's estate, and in arranging for the auction of his house and furnishings, I came across these things. I'm sure they belong to you. I was...shocked to discover them."

Deborah removed the lid. "My mink coat and jewelry," she said without surprise. "How did you know they were mine?"

"Well, I—I remember the chain and medallion. And, there was the monogram inside the coat. I was sure the *S* stood for Standridge. I also acted on a...horrible hunch and called the sheriff's department in that county where you used to live, and they still had a record of the items stolen. Those things were listed."

Deborah fingered the coat. "Then you know that Randall stole them?"

"Yes," he said shamefacedly. "And the drawings. I believe I've figured out why. It was a shock to me, Deborah, to discover after he died the kind of man he was, what he did to you."

"Did it take you that long?" Deborah asked ironically.

"I refused to see what I didn't want to see. I ... cared for him, you know. When he came to me that day and asked me to lie about the columns, I did it because I believed in him. He said he was working for your best interests, that he was protecting you from yourself."

"He didn't offer you my job to entice you to lie?" asked Deborah in surprise.

"No, of course not. He relied on my going along with him because he knew about my real feelings for you—"

"Your *real* feelings?"

"Yes," John stammered, turning red. "He knew that I—that I—had always admired you, and well, cared a great deal for you."

"What?" Deborah sat up on the edge of her seat. "John, you *hated* me!"

"No, Deborah." John swallowed, his prominent Adam's apple bobbing as he struggled with his words. "That was ... just a smoke screen to conceal my true feelings. I was resentful that you never looked at men like me. You only went out with men of importance, the successful ones who knew how to dress and what to say. You never gave anyone like me the time of day, and I—I felt affronted. None of them, not until Mr. Parker came along, could begin to feel for you what I did."

"John ..." Deborah went to sit beside him on the couch and laid a hand on his arm. "I am so sorry. You must never believe that I was indifferent to you for the reasons you thought. It's a long, long story, but one that I hope you'll give me the opportunity to tell you sometime. How have you been since Randall died?"

He shrugged, smiling slightly. "The same. Lonely. None of the original crew is with the firm anymore. Even Tony Pierson is gone. Randall drove everybody away. It was as if they were all a reminder of you. I think...he went a little crazy when both you and Bea left. I wonder now if he wasn't the one who torched your house in the foothills. Was the culprit ever found?"

"No," she answered, allowing him his doubts. She herself had none. In the mail several days after the fire had come the set of house keys Randall had used over Thanksgiving. They had been enfolded in a white sheet of blank paper containing ashes in the crease. "Because of the burglar bars, firemen were unable to save anything. That's why I'm especially appreciative of your bringing me these things."

"Do you miss your mountain?" he asked curiously.

"No." Deborah smiled, thinking, *I have my mountain*.

Through the wide front window, he had seen a school bus draw up to the house. Now there was a clamor in the hall. John turned to see two little boys being divested of overcoats and caps by Mrs. Watson, their voices piping and breathless.

"Come in here, boys," called their mother. "I have someone I'd like you to meet." She got up to greet them, her face aglow with a happiness that filled his heart with a strange contentment. He stood also. "Roger, Daniel, this is Mr. John Turner, an old...friend of your mother's," she said, glancing at John, who nodded in approval. "Mr. Turner and Aunt Bea and I used to work together."

The two little boys, husky reproductions of their father, shook hands solemnly. "Before you were our mommy?" asked Roger, the older.

"Yes, darling." She touched his hair. "Now you two may go get some cookies." They scampered off and Deborah said, "It's time to wake my daughter from her nap. I'd like you to meet her. And Dan should be in soon. Won't you stay awhile?"

"Oh no, no, no," said John hastily, wanting to stay. "Perhaps another time. I've got to get back to the office."

Deborah took his arm as she escorted him to the door. "Promise you'll come again, John. Shall we say next Thursday for dinner? I'll have Bea and Bill, too. You'll like Bill, and Bea would love to see you again. Do say yes."

"Deborah—" he said, suddenly extraordinarily happy. "I'd like that very much. Thank you."

He knew she watched him from the door as he hurried down the walk to his car, uncaring of the snow. He was glad he had come.

In the sweeping tradition of the *New York Times* bestselling *Roses*, Leila Meacham delivers another grand yet intimate novel set against the rich backdrop of early twentieth-century Texas. In the midst of this transformative time in Southern history, two unforgettable characters emerge and find their fates irrevocably intertwined as they love, lose, and betray.

TURN THE PAGE FOR A PREVIEW OF

TITANS

ON SALE NOW.

Prologue

From a chair beside her bed, Leon Holloway leaned in close to his wife's wan face. She lay exhausted under clean sheets, eyes tightly closed, her hair brushed and face washed after nine harrowing hours of giving birth.

"Millicent, do you want to see the twins now? They need to be nursed," Leon said softly, stroking his wife's forehead.

"Only one," she said without opening her eyes. "Bring me only one. I couldn't abide two. You choose. Let the midwife take the other and give it to that do-gooder doctor of hers. He'll find it a good home."

"Millicent—" Leon drew back sharply. "You can't mean that."

"I do, Leon. I can bear the curse of one, but not two. Do what I say, or so help me, I'll drown them both."

"Millicent, honey…it's too early. You'll change your mind."

"Do what I say, Leon. I mean it."

Leon rose heavily. His wife's eyes were still closed, her lips tightly sealed. She had the bitterness in her to do as she threatened, he knew. He left the bedroom to go downstairs to the kitchen where the midwife had cleaned and wrapped the crying twins.

"They need to be fed," she said, her tone accusatory. "The

idea of a new mother wanting to get herself cleaned up before tending to the stomachs of her babies! I never heard of such a thing. I've a mind to put 'em to my own nipples, Mr. Holloway, if you'd take no offense at it. Lord knows I've got plenty of milk to spare."

"No offense taken, Mrs. Mahoney," Leon said, "and...I'd be obliged if you *would* wet-nurse one of them. My wife says she can feed only one mouth."

Mrs. Mahoney's face tightened with contempt. She was of Irish descent and her full, lactating breasts spoke of the recent delivery of her third child. She did not like the haughty, reddish-gold-haired woman upstairs who put such stock in her beauty. She would have liked to express to the missy's husband what she thought of his wife's cold, heartless attitude toward the birth of her newborns, unexpected though the second one was, but the concern of the moment was the feeding of the child. She began to unbutton the bodice of her dress. "I will, Mr. Holloway. Which one?"

Leon squeezed shut his eyes and turned his back to her. He could not bear to look upon the tragedy of choosing which twin to feast at the breast of its mother while allocating the other to the milk of a stranger. "Rearrange their order or leave them the same," he ordered the midwife. "I'll point to the one you're to take."

He heard the midwife follow his instructions, then pointed a finger over his shoulder. When he turned around again, he saw that the one taken was the last born, the one for whom he'd hurriedly found a holey sheet to serve as a bed and covering. Quickly, Leon scooped up the infant left. His sister was already suckling hungrily at her first meal. "I'll be back, Mrs. Mahoney. Please don't leave. You and I must talk."

Chapter One

On the day Nathan Holloway's life changed forever, his morning began like any other. Zak, the German shepherd he'd rescued and raised from a pup, licked a warm tongue over his face. Nathan wiped at the wet wake-up call and pushed him away. "Aw, Zak," he said, but in a whisper so as not to awaken his younger brother, sleeping in his own bed across the room. Sunrise was still an hour away, and the room was dark and cold. Nathan shivered in his night shift. He had left his underwear, shirt, and trousers on a nearby chair for quiet and easy slipping into as he did every night before climbing into bed. Randolph still had another hour's sleep coming to him, and there would be hell to pay if Nathan disturbed his brother.

Socks and boots in hand and with the dog following, Nathan let himself out into the hall and sat on a bench to pull them on. The smell of bacon and onions frying drifted up from the kitchen. Nothing better for breakfast than bacon and onions on a cold morning with a day of work ahead, Nathan thought. Zak, attentive to his master's every move and thought, wagged his tail in agreement. Nathan chuckled softly and gave the animal's neck a quick, rough rub. There would be potatoes and hot biscuits with butter and jam, too.

His mother was at the stove, turning bacon. She was already dressed, hair in its neat bun, a fresh apron around her trim form. "G'morning, Mother," Nathan said sleepily, passing by her to hurry outdoors to the privy. Except for his sister, the princess, even in winter, the menfolks were discouraged from using the chamber pot in the morning. They had to head to the outhouse. Afterward, Nathan would wash in the mudroom off the kitchen where it was warm and the water was still hot in the pitcher.

"Did you wake your brother?" his mother said without turning around.

"No, ma'am. He's still sleeping."

"He's got that big test today. You better not have awakened him."

"No, ma'am. Dad about?"

"He's seeing to more firewood."

As Nathan quickly buttoned into his jacket, his father came into the back door with an armload of the sawtooth oak they'd cut and stacked high in the fall. "Mornin', son. Sleep all right?"

"Yessir."

"Good boy. Full day ahead."

"Yessir."

It was their usual exchange. All days were full since Nathan had completed his schooling two years ago. A Saturday of chores awaited him every weekday, not that he minded. He liked farmwork, being outside, alone most days, just him and the sky and the land and the animals. Nathan took the lit lantern his father handed him and picked up a much-washed flour sack containing a milk bucket and towel. Zak followed him to the outhouse and did his business in the dark perimeter of the woods while Nathan did his, then Nathan and the dog went to the barn to attend to his before-breakfast chores, the light from the lantern leading the way.

Daisy, the cow, mooed an agitated greeting from her stall. "Hey, old girl," Nathan said. "We'll have you taken care of in a minute." Before grabbing a stool and opening the stall gate, Nathan shone the light around the barn to make sure no unwanted visitor had taken shelter during the cold March night. It was not unheard of to find a vagrant in the hayloft or, in warmer weather, to discover a snake curled in a corner. Once a hostile, wounded fox had taken refuge in the toolshed.

Satisfied that none had invaded, Nathan hung up the lantern and opened the stall gate. Daisy ambled out and went directly to her feed trough, where she would eat her breakfast while Nathan milked. He first brushed the cow's sides of hair and dirt that might fall into the milk, then removed the bucket from the sack and began to clean her teats with the towel. Finally he stuck the bucket under the cow's bulging udder, Zak sitting expectantly beside him, alert for the first squirt of warm milk to relieve the cow's discomfort.

Daisy allowed only Nathan to milk her. She refused to cooperate with any other member of the family. Nathan would press his hand to her right flank, and the cow would obligingly move her leg back for him to set to his task. With his father and siblings, she'd keep her feet planted, and one of them would have to force her leg back while she bawled and trembled and waggled her head, no matter that her udder was being emptied. "You alone got the touch," his father would say to him.

That was all right by Nathan and with his brother and sister as well, two and three years behind him, respectively. They got to sleep later and did not have to hike to the barn in inclement weather before the sun was up, but Nathan liked this time alone. The scents of hay and the warmth of the animals, especially in winter, set him at ease for the day.

The milk collected, Nathan put the lid on the bucket and set it high out of Zak's reach while he fed and watered the horses and led the cow to the pasture gate to turn her out for grazing. The sun was rising, casting a golden glow over the brown acres of the Barrows homestead that would soon be awash with the first growth of spring wheat. It was still referred to as the Barrows farm, named for the line of men to whom it had been handed down since 1840. Liam Barrows, his mother's father, was the last heir to bear the name. Liam's two sons had died before they could inherit, and the land had gone to his daughter, Millicent Holloway. Nathan was aware that someday the place would belong to him. His younger brother, Randolph, was destined for bigger and better things, he being the smarter, and his sister, Lily, would marry, she being beautiful and already sought after by sons of the well-to-do in Gainesville and Montague and Denton, even from towns across the border in the Indian Territory. "I won't be living out my life in a calico dress and kitchen apron" was a statement the family often heard from his sister, the princess.

That was all fine by Nathan, too. He got along well with his siblings, but he was not one of them. His brother and sister were close, almost like twins. They had the same dreams—to be rich and become somebody—and were focused on the same goal: to get off the farm. At nearly twenty, Nathan had already decided that to be rich was to be happy where you were, doing the things you liked, and wanting for nothing more.

So it was that that morning, when he left the barn with milk bucket in hand, his thoughts were on nothing more than the hot onions and bacon and buttered biscuits that awaited him before

he set out to repair the fence in the south pasture after breakfast. His family was already taking their seats at the table when
he entered the kitchen. Like always, his siblings took chairs
that flanked his mother's place at one end of the table while he
seated himself next to his father's at the other. The family arrangement had been such as long as Nathan could remember:
Randolph and Lily and his mother in one group, he and his father in another. Like a lot of things, it was something he'd been
aware of but never noticed until the stranger appeared in the
late afternoon.

Chapter Two

The sun was behind him and sinking fast when Nathan stowed hammer and saw and nails and started homeward, carrying his toolbox and lunch pail. The sandwiches his mother had prepared with the extra bacon and onions and packed in the pail with pickles, tomato, and boiled egg had long disappeared, and he was hungry for his supper. It would be waiting when he returned, but it would be awhile before he sat down to the evening meal. He had Daisy to milk. His siblings would have fed the horses and pigs and chickens before sundown, so he'd have only the cow to tend before he washed up and joined the family at the table.

It was always something he looked forward to, going home at the end of the day. His mother was a fine cook and served rib-sticking fare, and he enjoyed the conversation around the table and the company of his family before going to bed. Soon, his siblings would be gone. Randolph, a high school senior, seventeen, had already been accepted at Columbia University in New York City to begin his studies, aiming for law school after college. His sister, sixteen, would no doubt be married within a year or two. How the evenings would trip along when they were gone, he didn't know. Nathan didn't contribute much to the gatherings. Like his father, his thoughts on things were seldom asked and almost never offered. He was merely a quiet listener, a fourth at cards and board games (his mother did not play), and a dependable source to bring in extra wood, stoke the fire, and replenish cups of cocoa. Still, he felt a part of the family scene if for the most part ignored, like the indispensable clock over the mantel in the kitchen.

Zak trotted alongside him unless distracted by a covey of doves to flush, a rabbit to chase. Nathan drew in a deep breath of the cold late-March air, never fresher than at dusk when the day had lost its sun and the wind had subsided, and expelled it with a sense of satisfaction. He'd had a productive day. His father would be pleased that he'd been able to repair the whole south fence and that the expense of extra lumber had been justified. Sometimes they disagreed on what needed to be done for the amount of the expenditure, but his father always listened to his son's judgment and often let him have his way. More times than not, Nathan had heard his father say to his mother, "The boy's got a head for what's essential for the outlay, that's for sure." His mother rarely answered unless it was to give a little sniff or utter a *humph*, but Nathan understood her reticence was to prevent him from getting a big head.

As if his head would ever swell over anything, he thought, especially when compared to his brother and sister. Nathan considered that everything about him—when he considered himself at all—was as ordinary as a loaf of bread. Except for his height and strong build and odd shade of blue-green eyes, nothing about him was of any remarkable notice. Sometimes, a little ruefully, he thought that when it came to him, he'd stood somewhere in the middle of the line when the good Lord passed out exceptional intellects, talent and abilities, personalities, and looks while Randolph and Lily had been at the head of it. He accepted his lot without rancor, for what good was a handsome face and winning personality for growing wheat and running a farm?

Nathan was a good thirty yards from the first outbuildings before he noticed a coach and team of two horses tied to the hitching post in front of the white wood-framed house of his home. He could not place the pair of handsome Thoroughbreds and expensive Concord. No one that he knew in Gainesville owned horses and carriage of such distinction. He guessed the owner was a rich new suitor of Lily's who'd ridden up from Denton or from Montague across the county line. She'd met several such swains a couple of months ago when the wealthiest woman in town, his mother's godmother, had hosted a little coming-out party for his sister. Nathan puzzled why he'd shown up to court her during the school week at this late hour of the day. His father wouldn't like that, not that he'd have much say in it. When it came to his sister, his mother had the last word, and she encouraged Lily's rich suitors.

Nathan had turned toward the barn when a head appeared above a window of the coach. It belonged to a middle-aged man who, upon seeing Nathan, quickly opened the door and hopped out. "I say there, me young man!" he called to Nathan. "Are ye the lad we've come to see?"

An Irishman, sure enough, and obviously the driver of the carriage, Nathan thought. He automatically glanced behind him as though half expecting the man to have addressed someone else. Turning back his gaze, he called, "Me?"

"Yes, you."

"I'm sure not."

"If ye are, ye'd best go inside. He doesn't like to be kept waiting."

"Who doesn't like to be kept waiting?"

214

"Me employer, Mr. Trevor Waverling."

"Never heard of him." Nathan headed for the barn.

"Wait! Wait!" the man cried, scrambling after him. "Ye must go inside, lad. Mr. Waverling won't leave until ye do." The driver had caught up with Nathan. "I'm cold and…me backside's shakin' hands with me belly. I ain't eaten since breakfast," he whined.

Despite the man's desperation and his natty cutaway coat, striped trousers, and stiff top hat befitting the driver of such a distinctive conveyance, Nathan thought him comical. He was not of particularly short stature, but his legs were not long enough for the rest of him. His rotund stomach seemed to rest on their trunks, no space between, and his ears and Irish red hair stuck out widely beneath the hat like a platform for a stovepipe. He reminded Nathan of a circus clown he'd once seen.

"Well, that's too bad," Nathan said. "I've got to milk the cow." He hurried on, curious of who Mr. Waverling was and the reason he wished to see him. If so, his father would have sent his farmhand to get him, and he must tend to Daisy.

The driver ran back to the house and Nathan hurried to the barn. Before he reached it, he heard Randolph giving Daisy a smack. "Stay still, damn you!"

"What are you doing?" Nathan exclaimed from the open door, surprised to see Randolph and Lily attempting to milk Daisy.

"What does it look like?" Randolph snapped.

"Get away from her," Nathan ordered. "That's my job."

"Let him do it," Lily pleaded. "I can't keep holding her leg back."

"We can't," Randolph said. "Dad said to send him to the house the minute he showed up."

His siblings often discussed him in the third person in his presence. Playing cards and board games, they'd talk about him as if he weren't sitting across the table from them. "Wonder what card he has," they'd say to each other. "Do you suppose he'll get my king?"

"Both of you get away from her," Nathan commanded. "I'm not going anywhere until I milk Daisy. Easy, old girl," he said, running a hand over the cow's quivering flanks. "Nathan is here."

Daisy let out a long bawl, and his brother and sister backed away. When it came to farm matters, after their father, Nathan had the top say.

"Who is Mr. Waverling, and why does he want to see me?" Nathan asked.

Brother and sister looked at each other. "We don't know," they both piped together, Lily adding, "But he's rich."

"We were sent out of the house when the man showed up," Randolph said, "but Mother and Dad and the man are having a shouting match over you."

"Me?" Nathan pulled Daisy's teats, taken aback. Who would have a shouting match over him? "That's all you know?" he asked. Zak had come to take his position at his knee and was rewarded with a long arc of milk into his mouth.

"That's all we know, but we think...we think he's come to take you away, Nathan," Lily said. Small, dainty, she came behind her older brother and put her arms around him, leaning into his back protectively. "I'm worried," she said in a small voice.

"Me, too," Randolph chimed in. "Are you in trouble? You haven't done anything bad, have you, Nathan?"

"Not that I know of," Nathan said. Take him away? What was this?

"What a silly thing to ask, Randolph," Lily scolded. "Nathan never does anything bad."

"I know that, but I had to ask," her brother said. "It's just that the man is important. Mother nearly collapsed when she saw him. Daddy took charge and sent us out of the house immediately. Do you have any idea who he is?"

"None," Nathan said, puzzled. "Why should I?"

"I don't know. He seemed to know about you. And you look like him...a little."

Another presence had entered the barn. They all turned to see their father standing in the doorway. He cleared his throat. "Nathan," he said, his voice heavy with sadness, "when the milkin's done, you better come to the house. Randolph, you and Lily stay here."

"But I have homework," Randolph protested.

"It can wait," Leon said as he turned to go. "Drink the milk for your supper."

The milking completed and Daisy back in her stall, Nathan left the barn, followed by the anxious gazes of his brother and sister. Dusk had completely fallen, cold and biting. His father had stopped halfway to the house to wait for him. Nathan noticed the circus clown had scrambled back into the carriage. "What's going on, Dad?" he said.

His father suddenly bent forward and pressed his hands to his face.

"Dad! What in blazes—?" Was his father crying? "What's the matter? What's happened?"

A tall figure stepped out of the house onto the porch. He paused, then came down the steps toward them, the light from the house at his back. He was richly dressed in an overcoat of fine wool and carried himself with an air of authority. He was a handsome man in a lean, wolfish sort of way, in his forties, Nathan guessed. "I am what's happened," he said.

Nathan looked him up and down. "Who are you?" he demanded, the question bored into the man's sea-green eyes, so like his own. He would not have dared, but he wanted to put his arm protectively around his father's bent shoulders.

"I am your father," the man said.

About the Author

Leila Meacham is a writer and former teacher who lives in San Antonio, Texas. She is the bestselling author of the novels *Roses*, *Tumbleweeds*, *Somerset*, *Titans, Ryan's Hand,* and *Aly's House*. For more information, you can visit LeilaMeacham.com.

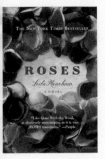

"Heralded as the new *Gone with the Wind*" (*USA Today*), this acclaimed novel brings back the epic storytelling that readers have always loved—in a panoramic saga of dreams, power struggles, and forbidden passions in East Texas...

The epic storytelling of *Roses* meets the moving drama of *Friday Night Lights* in this heartrending story of three friends who forge a lifelong bond against the backdrop of a Texas town's passion for football.

Gone with the Wind meets *The Help* in the stunning prequel to Leila Meacham's *New York Times* bestselling family epic, *Roses*.

A sweeping new drama of long-hidden secrets, enduring bonds, and redemption set in turn-of-the-century Texas.

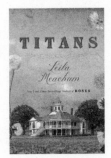